H.F. Danty is an author who began writing poetry at very young age. The author's continues love for writing led her to write stories later in life.

Late of 2018, she became curious about art and became an artist. Yet, writing poetry still remains too dear to her heart and writing stories is her escape from tough times.

For my mom, the love of my life, whom I miss the most.
For my siblings, whom I love dearly.
To my readers, thank you so much.

H.F. Danty

UNSPOKEN TALES: TRAILS TO THE TRUTH

AUSTIN MACAULEY PUBLISHERS™
LONDON • CAMBRIDGE • NEW YORK • SHARJAH

Copyright © H.F. Danty 2022

The right of H.F. Danty to be identified as author of this work has been asserted by the author in accordance with Federal Law No. (7) of UAE, Year 2002, Concerning Copyrights and Neighboring Rights.

All rights reserved. No part of this publication may be reproduced, stored in a retrieval system, or transmitted in any form or by any means, electronic, mechanical, photocopying, recording, or otherwise, without the prior permission of the publishers.

Any person who commits any unauthorized act in relation to this publication may be liable to legal prosecution and civil claims for damages.

This is a work of fiction. Names, characters, businesses, places, events, locales, and incidents are either the products of the author's imagination or used in a fictitious manner. Any resemblance to actual persons, living or dead, or actual events is purely coincidental.

The age group that matches the content of the books has been classified according to the age classification system issued by the National Media Council.

ISBN – 9789948817123 – (Paperback)
ISBN – 9789948817130 – (E-Book)

Application Number: MC-10-01-4349028
Age Classification: 13+

Printer Name: iPrint Global Ltd
Printer Address: Witchford, England

First Published 2022
AUSTIN MACAULEY PUBLISHERS FZE
Sharjah Publishing City
P.O Box [519201]
Sharjah, UAE
www.austinmacauley.ae
+971 655 95 202

1- Sunset of New Beginnings

The sun's journey came to an end once again and its colors lay down across the sea, resting after a long day. Ready to leave the sky into the water, while a little boy sat down on the golden shores painting the view in front of him. He might not be the best at it but he surely observed it better; to a moment he was lost in the view, thinking, *I wonder if I'd swim toward the horizon, would I find a chest filled with gold?*

A few minutes passed and he realized the colors changed in front of him and became different than the ones he painted with on his paper. He picked his brush again and tried to paint the rest; however, a warm hand rested on his shoulder; interrupting him from continuing his humble art.

He looked up and he saw the woman whom he believed the prettiest in the world, his mother.

"Here you are," his mother said with a smile.

"Mother!"

"I knew I would find you here."

"Yes, my father could arrive in any moment. I know he'd be here."

His mother's smile quickly faded away and was not sure how to respond to her son. She paused for a few moments and finally said, "Well, I told you to be home before sunset and you gave me your word to be home, right?"

"But Mother… I—"

"No. No excuses now, honey. Come on, now. You can always continue painting in your room."

Arthur sighed and he collected his stuff and put them in his leathered bag. He looked at his mother and noticed her sadness. She failed this time to cover her worries with a smile as she gazed at the sea with a hope for her husband's return.

At that very moment, Arthur understood his mother was not at her best and that he needed to transfer some strength to his lovely mother and for that, he held his mother's hand tightly.

"Mother, let's go home," Arthur said with a confident voice.

Arthur's father and his close friend had gone missing for almost two weeks. They never received a letter and nobody really said anything about him since. Except for some stories. Some said, Mr. Byron and his friend Jason fell off the fishing boat on the darkest night and drowned. Some said, the ocean monster ate them. Some said, they didn't see them on the boat. While Mrs. Byron knew for sure he was on the boat with the others and many saw him getting on the boat. She felt there was something wrong between the lines they spoke but she never knew what it was. Yet, deep inside, she believed her husband Edward was alive.

Arthur and his mother arrived home and they saw Patricia standing by their door. Arthur didn't like Patricia and he secretly called her a witch because whenever she'd hear news, she would spread it to the neighbors in a magical speed and she never cared if the news were correct or wrong. Some families or friends broke apart because of her.

"Hello, Patricia. It is good to see you."

"Hello, Medlee, I got some news about your husband."

"Oh goodness. I hope they're good," Medlee said while opening the door.

Arthur stood aside and let his mother and Patricia enter before him while looking at his own feet. He always remembered his father's words to him, "True gentlemen never enter a place before a lady. He has to stand aside and look at his feet. Every woman deserves to be respected and they shall walk in the place first. This is one of little things a gentleman should do." Those words echoed into Arthur's ears. He missed his father so much, and somehow remembering his words brought him a little comfort each time.

He entered the house. Patricia and his mother were already seated.

"Come on, tell me."

Patricia looked at Medlee then looked at Arthur and again at Medlee. Medlee understood Patricia's gesture.

"Arthur, please go to your room."

"I…" Arthur tried to say something but he couldn't argue about it. "Excuse me," he said. He went to his bedroom; however, he didn't close the door well and stood by it; hoping to hear what they'd say. His bedroom's door was actually broken; like sometimes if the front door was shut strongly, his door would open up if it wasn't locked up with the key.

"Alright, now I shall speak."

"Please speak up, you're killing me inside."

"Patience, Medlee, have a little patience. I will speak right away. Your husband and his friend Jason were seen somewhere not too far."

"Where?!"

"In Rubia. I'm sorry to tell you this but," Patricia looked at the table with a little evil grin on her face and finally looked up at Medlee's face, "they saw them with two women in the shops."

"Stop. Don't say another single word," Medlee hit the table and stood up. "I don't allow nonsense spoken in my house. IN MY HUSBAND'S HOUSE." She rose her arm and aimed toward the door "Here is the door, I don't want to hear more. The door is open."

Patricia stood up with a big shook on her face and pity laughter in her heart. "You're kicking me out? Is this how you treat your neighbors?"

"Please walk on."

"I will leave but listen, let the days prove one of us right."
"Leave already!" Medlee shouted.

Once she left, Medlee slammed the front door and Arthur bedroom's door opened up widely. Poor little Arthur, he didn't have the habit of eavesdropping. It was his very first time. He froze in his spot with a thundering heart, it was beating fast as if he had just run around the neighborhood barefoot twice. His mother glared at him; she spoke nothing but the house felt it was on fire. She sighed, and finally went to her bedroom. Arthur wiped the sweat off his forehead with his arm. He felt bad about his doing. But he couldn't help it. He wanted to know about what happened to his father badly.

Days passed and awful rumors were spreading all over the place about Arthur's father and his friend. Kids were pointing at Arthur and making fun of him, calling his father with names and at this point Arthur would defend and spoke well about his father in front of them all, yet none of them did believe him.

"He was always faithful to his family and this land. Stop calling my father with nasty names."

Kids didn't stop the jokes. Arthur's attitude had changed and he started fighting with other boys. Pushing them off and punching them in the face. He kept doing this whenever the boys would say a bad word about his dear father.

Until one day, his mother caught him fighting and dragged him out of the fight. Boys were laughing at him and he was too embarrassed. His mother continued pulling him from his hand and walked in hurry. He didn't say anything and neither did his mother.

They were very close to arriving home and Arthur stared up at the sky. It was a cloudy day yet there was this strange thing. There was a dark grey cloud over their house, leaving a huge shade. He noticed it earlier. It stayed over there for a long time but refused to move nor to rain. That sort of weather made him worried.

They entered the house and right away they headed to the basement. Arthur got scared. He guessed this was going to be a punishment for him to be locked up in the basement with rats since he had heard such stories from the other kids in the neighborhood before.

His mother let go of his hand. She held her chain which was around her neck and took off a key. She grabbed a match from her pocket and lighted up a long candle. She gently held Arthur's hand and his worries slowly faded away once they entered the basement and quickly turned into a surprise.

"Wow. What is this place?" Arthur said and his mouth stayed open. He tried to look at everything around him and not to miss a thing. "We had a place like this The WHOLE TIME?"

The basement looked like a library, like the one at his school but smaller and neater. Arthur surely loved it.

"Son," his mother said and bent down to be almost his height. "You see all these books? These books belonged to your father."

She paused for a moment and she could see the excitement on her son's face as he looked around.

"History books, tales and poetry. Not only the books he purchased and collected but also there are some journals he wrote during some of his journeys," she stood still and took a few steps and said, "look, like this journal."

His mother grabbed a leather notebook.

"Can I have it? Please, please?" Arthur demanded.

"Mhm… but I have some conditions."

Without hesitation, Arthur asked, "What are they?"

"First condition, you must promise me you won't fight with other kids again."

"Mother… How am I supposed to protect myself then?"

"You were not protecting yourself, son. You were the one who started the fight."

"I didn't, Mother, they said bad things about my father."

"They said but they didn't punch you, did they?"

"No, they didn't."

"Then it's you who started the fight."

"I'm sorry," Arthur said without denying further.

"Did you change your mind? I can put this notebook back on the bookshelf and we can forget about the whole thing."

"No, Mother. I promise you. I will never start a fight again."

"Promise me like a gentleman. Stand still, look me in the eye and keep your head up. Now, promise me."

Arthur straightened his back like a solider was going to fight in a war; he kept his head up and looked at his mother in the eye.

He cleared his throat and finally said, "I promise you, like a gentleman does. I will never fight the other boys because gentlemen don't get their hands dirty in a fight."

"Exactly! That's my son. Now, my second condition; you must promise me you wouldn't take any of these books and any of your father's journals outside the house. Never show them to anyone."

"I promise you. I will read them alone and I will read them inside the house."

"I trust you, my son. Now here, take this notebook and go read it in your bedroom."

Ever since then, reading became a passion for Arthur and a peaceful land for his mind. He found comfort especially when he'd read his father's journals. He felt he was speaking to him through his written words.

Arthur became the calm kid he used to be. With time, he found out there was something he could enjoy beside reading which was writing! Mrs. Ritz taught them to write and in one of the classes he took, she taught them how to write a letter. Once he learned writing, he didn't stop doing it. He wrote about his daily life and letters – well, TONS of letters for his father to the point his mother had to do something about it. She asked him to continue writing but not every day. She couldn't afford buying many papers since she got paid less at some days when she didn't get many demands for sewing dresses. She told him to only write important events of his life. "Write about something special that happened to you. Something unusual. And also, how about you write your father a letter or two yearly, telling him how you spent the year in short."

Arthur understood the situation and he was shifting between reading and writing with a sort of balance.

After a while, people stopped saying much about Arthur's father because this strange thing happened again and again. Men would disappear when they reached the ocean and sometimes, they'd be found dead by the shore. There was a feeling of horror spreading all over the town. The old chief had to send a messenger with a letter to the king, telling him about this tragic thing that kept happening. Shortly after, the king had some doubts that could be a sign for another war from the West. He prepared an army and battleships. Yet, no attacks happened. He sent a messenger to the West, specifically to Shellia, with a word of peace.

Shellia's queen sent a letter to the king with a word of peace as well and wanting to pay a visit to Lillianta for a meeting. That truly happened and big ceremonies took place expecting Shellia's queen and the prince's arrival. Everyone gathered by the sea port with warm greetings. Arthur and his mother attended that event but poor Arthur, he only saw people's legs and feet as he was still quite small. His mother wasn't able to see much either except for the fancy carriage passing by.

The meeting took place and people got to know that same thing was happening in the land of Shellia. Fishermen or sailors would disappear or be found dead. Both parties made sure they came for peace and they perhaps had the same enemy to fight against.

*

For some time, Lillianta had quiet and peaceful times. In another hand, the hard times kept repeating themselves again, taking away the silence and peace once in a while.

But time passed on. Years felt unnoticeable and passed as fast as the thunder. Young men became wise, old men retired from their jobs and stayed home. A new chief had taken the position. Houses needed new paint and kids needed new clothes as they grew up fast. And Arthur stayed the same, he kept his soul clean and it seemed some of his habits remained the same, no matter how the time had quickly passed.

To be exact, ten years passed. Arthur had finished his studies and he was now a gentleman of age 17, sitting at the table writing his yearly letter for his father.

Dear Father,

I wish you would come home any day and any minute soon. I wish you're in a good health and I hope you're thinking of us every day as we always do.

Today, I mark this day as it is a big day for me that I wish you to be here with me. I finished my studies. I wish you could see me and be proud of me.

I have always wanted to be a teacher and sometimes I want to be a wanderer or a fisherman like you. Yet, the hardship of life didn't allow me to be one of which I desired. No worries now, Father.

I have two jobs and I believe we can hold on and see better days ahead. As I'd make more money for my mother and me.

I pray the Lord to have your arrival sooner and live together like how we used to be. I believe you're alive somewhere and I pray you don't suffer wherever you are. I will try my best on my side to find clues and trails to find you if your arrival would delay further. I am a man now and I do see myself be able to travel and sail the sea. Nobody knows how we'd meet but if taking a step forward to find you, will ease your return, I'm ready to take the risk.

Wherever you are, I pray for you and always will love you.

Your only son,
Arthur Byron

"Arthur, when will you quit this habit of writing on the dining table while you have your own desk at your room? And… and why all these papers when you only need one?" his mother said.

Arthur shrugged and rubbed his head. He covered his embarrassment with a little laugh.

She sighed and smiled at him. "Honey, the dinner is ready. Please gather your stuff off the table."

"I will pick them up right away! But I got to say this. The smell of the pumpkin soup is mmm, fantastic."

The whole house smelled like pumpkin soup and in fact Arthur was writing his letter with a growling stomach. He was almost, once, about to write pumpkin in his letter by mistake.

"Thanks, dear. I hope you'd enjoy it too."

"I surely will."

He collected all his things and went to his bedroom. He placed his pens and papers on his desk. Then, he finally put his letter into an envelope and put it inside a large box which filled with other letters and journals.

"I served the soup," his mother said and at same moment, somebody knocked on the door loudly and continuously. The first thought that came to Arthur's mind was *Could this be my father?* since he had just written the letter, his father was still on his mind and also nobody had knocked on their door like this serious for a long time.

Arthur and his mother rushed toward the door; however, his mother managed to open it first.

It was Mr. Barden spreading the news in the neighborhood, walking forward and backward to make sure everyone heard the news. "Everybody, news, news. Gather up by the seashore. Twelve men were found by the seashore. Please, gather up by the seashore. Tell your family and friends. News, news…"

People were talking loud in the neighborhood. Arthur was shocked and remained silent. *No, my father shouldn't be one of them. Please, God, don't let this happen to me.* Those words were repeating inside his mind. He finally looked at his mother. She was still holding the door open and she placed her hand on her heart for a few moments. Suddenly, she ran out of the house. Arthur ran after her.

"MOTHER! STOP!"

She slowed down to take off her pair of shoes to run faster. Her scarf fell off her shoulders. Arthur would stop each time to pick up her shoes… her scarf… They were running with other people along the wooden houses, Carling's Bakery, Alvin's butcher… more buildings and trees passed by. Shops were left open without their owners staying. The whole town left their places to go to the seashore in madness and horror.

For almost three years, such news like this hadn't been heard. People believed those who were gone could have passed away and nobody would ever go missing after them. Which now was proved wrong.

Arthur tried to pass through the crowd and he kept saying "Excuse me" many times.

"Everybody, please stay back. Only the families who had a missing member of their families stand in the line. The rest of you, stand back. Excuse me, sir, you know someone's missing in your family… no? Then go back. I repeat, only those who had…"

Arthur finally made it to the front of the crowd and he looked at the line. He saw his mother was the last one standing in the line, so far. He tried to catch his breath after all the running. Yet, his heart was still jumping not because of the running but because he was afraid to see his father among the dead. He thought to himself, *I can't go there. I don't want the first dead body I see to happen to be my father's.*

His mother looked behind, trying to find Arthur but she was too stressful to see him. He rose his hand and waved it for her to notice him. He called her and she finally saw him. She moved her hand – giving him a gesture to come and join her. He nodded his head and took a deep breath. He tried his best to act like he was not worried, to comfort her. He walked towards her and patted on her shoulder.

"I'm here. Don't worry." he said. He placed his mother's shoes on the ground and helped her to wear them. He then gave her scarf.

Some families didn't recognize the bodies but few did and they were weeping loudly. The closer their turn got, the louder the weeping voices were heard. Arthur's eyes were burning, trying to hold back the tears, even though he hadn't yet seen the bodies. He was breaking inside for those who cried and he thought for a second… *What if my father is one of them…? After all those years of waiting…*

It was then their turn. Arthur didn't want to move forward but a part of him wanted to go fast to get to know. His mother froze. "Mother? It is our turn."

"I know… I know…" Yet she wasn't taking a step forward.

"Medlee… Arthur… come here," a familiar voice was calling for them. It was Medlee's brother; the new chief.

Medlee ran toward her brother and hugged him; mumbling over his shoulder, "I can't see the bodies… I cannot. Please tell me, is he alive?"

He held her in his arms. Arthur stood close to them. "Yes, sister… Yes. Edward could be still alive." Then he looked at Arthur and said, "Your father wasn't found among the dead."

Medlee stopped hugging his brother to thank God; "God, thank you. Thank you. I knew it. I put my trust in you. Thank you, God," Medlee said while looking up at the sky and tears washing her face.

Arthur was smiling with tearful eyes. He gave his mother a hug.

After that, Arthur's uncle walked with them all the way back to their home. Once they arrived, he excused himself.

"Tryess. No, come join us at the dinner."

"No, sis. I have to go. I still have lots to do. Leave it for another time."

"Right, you must be busy with all this mess. God be with you but come and visit us sometime. Bring your wife with you too next time."

"I will. You two take care. I must go now. Bye."

"Bye," Arthur and his mother said.

They both entered the house. Silence hit all over the place. Arthur felt it was too quiet, like he could hear their footsteps loudly in the house. Cold soup on the table, curtains-covered windows allowing a dim light. His mother placed her scarf heavily on the chair. She looked like she was carrying mountains on her shoulders. The news didn't make her happy neither sad. She felt a heaviness in her heart. Thinking of these people that were in sorrow today and at the same time she was thinking why she never received a letter from her husband until now. She had mixed feelings, yet she found a sort of comfort to know he wasn't one of those who were found dead. She still had a hope to see him again.

She slowly grabbed the bowls. Arthur took his bowl from her hand. "It is okay, Mother. I can eat it while it's cold."

"No! I will reheat the food," she insisted. Arthur let go of the bowl and let his mother do as she desired. He didn't want to upset her.

She went to the kitchen which was actually in the living room. Their house was small; their living room was their dining room and kitchen. Arthur wasn't sure what to do meanwhile and then it came to his mind; the idea to breathe fresh air in the backyard.

"Mother, I will go to the backyard for a little while."

"Sure, son."

He opened up the door to the backyard and the sky was all red. It was sunset time but Arthur had never seen the sky as this red. It looked like the sky was burning or bleeding. It was terrifying to watch. He got worried thinking what could happen next? Could there be sort of worse times coming on the way? But then he tried to shake his worries right away; remembering a quote he read in his father's journals. "Sunsets are new beginnings of a life, and of a journey. It's true the sun goes down but the moon will have its turn to start its journey. Then a new day starts again with a sunrise. And we shall start a new chapter – a new day too."

As Arthur remembered those words, he prayed for a better tomorrow.

2- Little Lie

Arthur stood on a top of a green hill. It was his first time to be in such a place like this. It felt chilly and windy. The wind made waves through the long grass and sunflowers. They looked like they were being tickled or perhaps swaying into a dance with the wind. Arthur looked up at the sky and he saw a big bird. No, a HUGE bird. It was surely not a falcon neither an eagle. It was triple the size of an eagle. Golden and shining bird, reflecting the sunlight in a sort of way. Suddenly, everything started to shake. An earthquake! Arthur tried to run but everything was falling apart. He tried to hold onto a rock or catch anything to prevent him from falling and he fell… on his bed.

He gasped as he woke up from this sweet dream that had turned into a nightmare by the end.

"I am sorry, honey. I didn't mean to scare you. I was trying to wake you up," his mother said while caressing his forehead and hair.

Arthur looked at his mother and then looked around. He found himself in his room, trying to manage to be back to his current life.

"Thank God, it was only a dream. But Mother, did you push me?"

"Yes, sorry. I called you and you didn't wake up. I pushed you gently to wake you up. Didn't want you to be late for work."

She pushed me gently… She has no idea; she shook off the hill in my dream, he thought.

"No worries. I will get up now. I'm wide awake."

"Okay then," his mother said and left the room.

It is a new day. It can be promising, Arthur thought as he got up. He went to the bathroom which was outside in the backyard to wash his face. He never like the idea of having the bathrooms in the backyard, and he hated it the most when it was winter. So cold to go out for the bathroom. He was thankful it was not winter yet. He sometimes wished he could change the designs and wished to have a word with whoever thought this was as a good idea.

He got himself ready and dressed up. He grabbed his glass of milk which was filled halfway. Some days, they couldn't offer to buy a big bottle of milk. So, they'd share the small bottle in half. As Arthur now had two jobs, there were some chances ahead to buy more supplies for the house soon.

He drank his milk while standing and took a big bite of his ginger cookie.

"Arthur, sit down and eat."

"I cannot. I'm—" he drank the last few drops out of his glass, "I'm afraid to be late."

"Gosh, Arthur, you're not even letting me have breakfast in peace." She got up and cut a loaf of bread in half and filled it with the last piece of cheese they had.

Arthur finished eating his cookie.

"I am done, I have to go."

"Wait, let me put this in your bag," his mother said. She wrapped the half loaf of bread filled with cheese in a paper and put it into his bag.

"You didn't finish your breakfast. At least eat that when you get hungry."

"Thank you, Mother," he grabbed his bag. "I shall go now. Bye."

"Take care. May God be with you."

Arthur walked in steady and fast steps. He looked at the people and observed their faces. They looked a bit calm today. Three days had passed since the big funeral for the loss of twelve men. People were sad. Some didn't even open their shops. They wouldn't say hello neither good morning but today, they greeted Arthur as he walked by with a pale smile. Time would heal people or perhaps people would get used to the pain as time passed.

Arthur got two jobs. He used to only work at Jones's Stables in afternoons but since he finished his studies, he got another job to do in the morning at a leather shop or tannery which was owned by his friend's father, Mr. Lomar.

Arthur opened the door.

"Good morning, Arthur. You came on time," Mr. Lomar said.

"Good morning, sir."

"Today, we have lots of work. I received cows' hides yesterday afternoon and I put them in the lime yard for a night and soaked them and I washed them in order to loosen the hair. All I need you to do is to remove all the hair off."

"Yes, will do. Anything else, sir?"

"Once you're done, I need you to continue making the belts that you didn't finish yesterday. And I'll handle the leather in the tannery with Peter."

"Sure thing. Excuse me, Mr. Lomar."

"You're excused."

Arthur left the shop. He went to the tannery which was a little far from the shop. Mr. Lomar would have to find another place for the tannery because… the smell. Arthur got a napkin out from his pocket and wrapped it over his nose and mouth and tied it well. The people complained a lot about the smell coming from the tannery. Therefore, Mr. Lomar had been looking for another place for the tannery lately. He was also thinking to expand his business. So, he was probably looking for a big new place. Arthur opened up the door of tannery and his stomach as usual started to act up at the beginning from just looking at the hides and also the smell that wouldn't be completely gone from the wrapped napkin over his face.

Arthur wore an apron and thick gloves, then he lifted up a hide and placed it on a wooden table. He picked up a blade, angled it back, and squeezed against its beam and pushed it over the skin to remove the hair off the hide. He needed to repeat the steps to make sure the hair were totally removed. He looked at other hides and he started to feel tired. *Seems like we have lots of work to do today,* he thought.

He picked up another hide. Shortly after, Peter arrived with his father Mr. Lomar with more hides.

"Hey, Arthur," Peter said in a very low tone as he was breathless from the heaviness of the hides they were carrying.

"Hey, buddy," Arthur replied.

They took the hides into the lime yard and then came back.

"I will handle the hides now. Arthur, once you're done with removing the hair, help Peter and carry the hides with him to be tanned. There's no time for making belts today," Mr. Lomar said.

"Will do," Peter and Arthur said.

"One more thing; if you two know anyone who wants to work in the tannery, let me know. I need to hire one or two more people," Mr. Lomar demanded.

"Okay, we will let you know," Peter said.

"All right," Mr. Lomar said and went to the lime yard.

"Hey, Arthur, did you know that Billy is back?" Peter said.

"Billy is in town? Since when?" Arthur asked surprisingly.

"Yes, he and his family came back last night. I didn't see him yet. Would you like to go with me to see him in the lunch break?"

"Sure thing. We can take Robert with us too."

"Yes… If Robert is in a good mood today."

"I think Robert will feel better to see us all gathered again with Billy."

"I hope so."

Peter, Billy, Robert, and Arthur became a group of friends five years ago. Before that, Arthur became friends with each of them individually. He had been friends with Robert for the longest time; they had been friends since Arthur was eight years old and Robert was nine years old. Despite the fact that both of their parents weren't always friendly with each other, yet Arthur and Robert's friendship blossomed. Arthur couldn't forget the time, when two kids tried to bully him and Robert stood up for him and even fought them off. Ever since then, they had become good friends. Robert was 18 years old now; a blond, muscular, tall guy – he was taller than Arthur and Peter. For many girls, he was their prince charming, yet he didn't fall for any of them.

Arthur met Billy when he was 12 years old and Billy was 14. They met in the library of the school and it so happened that they both wanted to borrow the same book. Without any hesitation, Billy let Arthur borrow the book first. After seeing each other in the library a few times and talking about the books they had read, eventually they became friends. Billy was 19 years old now; he's the tallest among his friends, had black hair and thin frame. He seemed to be an introvert but he had lots to say at times.

Peter was a little trouble maker when he was a child, he even bullied Arthur a few times but not for long. Arthur and Peter were class fellows but only became friends when both of them were 12 years old. Peter, of course, apologized for his foolishness when he was a little boy and he asked Arthur if he could forget the past and be friends. Surely, Arthur accepted that. Peter was now 17 years old, the same age as Arthur; he was the shortest in the group, thin but a little muscular, had black hair. Peter was an extrovert yet when a girl asked him for directions of a place, he'd forget the words to speak. He had low self-esteem when he would meet a girl, he'd think of himself as ugly even though he wasn't an ugly guy at all. He had many crushes and he never confessed to any of them.

Now as Billy was in town again, they finally could be reunited. Billy was away for about one month. He was a bookworm and for quite a while he had this bad habit of reading in a dim light at night. His sight was getting worse and he'd get headaches that were unbearable. Billy's family decided to see an eye doctor in Serina.

Meanwhile, Robert was not doing so well himself either. He was physically healthy but not so much emotionally. He had lost his father lately; he was one of the people who were found dead by the shore. Arthur and Peter were visiting him for the past three days but he wasn't into any conversation. However, they both hoped he'd feel a little better today if he went to meet Billy with them.

Arthur's shift of work was done for today and Peter took a break from work in order to visit Robert and Billy.

They went into the neighborhood where Billy and Robert lived. Peter started to fix his shirt while they were walking to make sure he looked alright. Because the rich and upper class lived in these neighborhoods; they had big wooden houses, front gardens and backyards. A married couple walked by who were wearing fancy clothes, they looked like they were going to attend a party or an important visit. And finally, they arrived at Robert's house.

"You knock on the door," Peter said.

"No, you knock on the door," said Arthur.

"No, you do…"

"Why me? You do it."

And Robert opened up the door. "Guys, I could hear your voices. Why this hesitation?"

"Nah, nothing… Hi," Peter said and he hit Arthur's arm with his elbow. He told him in a quiet voice, "Say hello."

"Hello. Hi, Robert," Arthur said.

"Guys, seriously… When will you stop being awkward? I'm okay now, alright?" Robert said.

"Are you sure?" Peter said.

Arthur hit Peter back with his elbow and he whispered to him, "Don't ask stupid questions now."

"It's okay, Arthur. I can hear your whisperings, guys. If you don't stop it, I'll close the door on you and don't come back like this," Robert said.

"No, sorry…" Arthur said.

"Okay. What now?" Robert asked.

"We're going to see Billy. Would you like to see him with us?" Peter requested.

"He's in town? Yes, of course, man. Let's go now," Robert responded.

On their way to see Billy, surprisingly, Robert was talking easily with them. He had been too quiet the past few days. Arthur had lots of questions in his mind regarding Robert; *Has he really moved on? Or is he just hiding his sadness within? But either way, I hope he's not keeping his sadness inside, because it can get worse with time.*

Soon, they arrived at Billy's house and everyone was excited to knock on the door. Peter and Robert couldn't decide who should be the one to knock on the door. As they were arguing together, Arthur stepped up and knocked on the door.

"Gosh, you're irritating, Arthur! You ruined this for us," Robert complained.

"I was going to knock on the door first," Peter said.

"No, I was going to," Robert argued back.

"Seriously, guys. You can argue forev—" Arthur was cut mid-sentence once Billy opened the door.

Billy looked a bit different. He was wearing something over his eyes that Arthur was amazed at but also found funny. For him, it looked like a mask, framed well but they were transparent, made of glass. Billy's eyes looked bigger through them. Arthur wondered if Billy actually saw them magnified as well. Everyone paused, looking at how Billy looked like.

"Hello friends. It's good to see you all again." Billy said.

They burst into laughter. Robert couldn't hold himself, he got on his knees while laughing out loud.

Arthur was trying hard to stop laughing. "What…" he chuckled. "What are you…" he chuckled again. "What are you wearing on your face?"

"Oh, these are glasses. Vision glasses."

"How can you wear glasses? Aren't they more useful for beverages?" Peter made fun of Billy and Robert laughed over the joke.

Arthur could see Billy's face was starting to blush. He was embarrassed.

Arthur personally hadn't seen anyone wearing glasses before in his life. The town he lived in was small and his family hardly traveled somewhere. Actually never.

"Can I touch them?" Arthur asked.

"Sure, but please be gentle." Billy handed Arthur his glasses.

Arthur looked at them carefully and tapped on the glasses gently. "Guys, they're really made of glass."

"Man, you're so naive. Of course, it is made of glass. You cannot be for real," Robert spoke.

"It is just that I have never met someone wearing these before," Arthur replied.

"Yeah, right. I forgot you live under a rock," Robert said.

Arthur felt ashamed. He thought it wasn't only him in the group that hadn't seen glasses before.

Peter grabbed Billy's glasses from Arthur's hand and wore them.

"Seriously… How can you see through that…? I see the world ruined through them," Peter commented.

"Peter, give them back to me. I can barely see anything without them," Billy said.

Peter let Arthur hold the glasses again and he looked through them. From just one look, his head started to spin. The view through them looked like everything was messed up, as if Arthur was in a tornado and everything was destroyed.

Robert came closer to them and grabbed the glasses and wore them but right away, he took them off.

"Man, how can you wear this? I got a headache right away from wearing them for a moment," Robert said and gave them back to Billy.

"Finally, you guys finished testing them out? That was not funny. I barely see anything without them, I am not joking," Billy said with a serious tone.

"And we can't see with them," Peter said.

Robert and Arthur laughed about it and then they all finally greeted Billy. Poor Billy, they always teased him but he always accepted their annoying jokes with a smiling heart.

They strolled and talked together. Robert mentioned to them about going on a trip. Maybe he wanted to go away for a bit to clear his mind but he suggested for them to go with him. Everyone accepted to go with him right away without hesitation, except for Arthur; because first, he needed to get permission from his mother to go and secondly, he needed to ask Mr. Jones to give him two days off. Peter said he'd ask his father Mr. Lomar to give them two days off. Arthur doubted that his father would allow them to get a short vacation as they were the only workers at his tannery and his leather shop even though sometimes Robbie, Peter's younger brother, stayed in the leather shop after school. Arthur was not sure if this would work out. However, the real problem was his mother. He knew she would say no for sure because his friends wanted to go to Rubia... Rubia was actually a nice place but the people here mostly thought of Rubia as a bad place. It had a bad reputation where everything was allowed, there was no ruler and no rules. Lillianta had rules that nobody dared to break.

Out of the blue, men started to walk in a rush to the local restaurant and they overheard them saying that the chief; Tryess Faylen (Arthur's uncle) was having a meeting and was prepared to make a speech there for all the men of the town. Arthur and his friends followed the people there but they couldn't enter the place because according to other men, they were too young to attend those meetings. So, they just decided to stand outside, little far away, and hear what the chief had to say.

"I say it one more time. We shall not be quiet about this, no more. We must stop this. We must have no fear to go to the ocean. Our land is lacking fish resources. The river and the sea, you may know the truth, if we continue fishing there, some type of fish will vanish; they will be extinct. We gave a warning two months ago that fishing was prohibited for a limited time but fishermen didn't hear a word. Now, we're suffering from this. If you, fishermen; you, gentlemen, didn't stop. We won't eat any fish anymore in the future. Therefore, I suggest you and all to go to the ocean and stop fishing in the near sea and the near rivers."

"The ocean! The ocean!" everyone said in a panic.

"Yes, the ocean, gentlemen. The ocean shall not stop us anymore. Don't you want to take revenge for our loss too? For the missing people whom we don't know if they're alive or dead? For the weaken hearts that wait every day and every year to have their loved ones come back home? Whatever the tales that have been told about the ocean and whatever the tales that have been told about Oernatus kingdom, the abandoned land… the cursed land. It shall not stop us. If the Oernatus land still exists and if it's the one that is responsible for the damage, we shall not be silent. We must fight. And if Oernatus is gone, then it's gone. And if you think that ocean's monster tale is real, do you then believe in myths? Nobody does. If you just fear the ocean, why are you afraid of it? It's ocean, it's just water, just like sea but bigger and deeper… Why do we need to fear if both are just salted water? Why do we fear it? Where are the brave hearts? Did the brave hearts die?"

"No, no," everyone shouted.

"I hear you here. You exist bravely and we need to show our braveness clearly. It's time to rebuild the *Maxemus* ship, our ocean fighter."

"Aye aye," everyone shouted.

"Those are not just words. They should become actions. I received a letter from General Chris Black that our king, His Highness Williams Afton gave the command to rebuild the warrior *Maxemus* ship. Let's get started from today…"

Once he finished his speech, everyone was shaking hands with the chief and Arthur and his friends hid away, watching the people as they left the place. Arthur's uncle saw them from afar and he came toward them. Arthur stood still in order to show his uncle that he had done nothing wrong while being there to listen to his speech, even though he was foolishly hiding some moments ago.

"Here's my nephew. How long have you been here?" He looked behind the wall. "And your friends too?"

They showed themselves up and stood beside Arthur after saying hello to him.

"We were here for quite a while," Arthur said.

"I assume you heard my speech," his uncle said.

"Yes, sir," Arthur answered.

"Why didn't you all enter in?" Chief Faylen asked.

"They don't allow us in and it was too crowded too. We stood behind with the other men," Peter said.

"Did someone stop you?" Chief Faylen asked him.

"No, sir," Peter said.

"Well, no one shall stop you anymore. You are all adults now and you should act like men, not hide here like kids," said Chief Faylen.

"Right," Peter said.

"Alright, I have to go now," said Arthur's uncle.

"Uncle... I mean, Chief. I need to talk to you about something," Arthur requested.

"Sure thing, come with me and we shall talk," his uncle said.

Arthur excused himself and told his friends to meet him in late afternoon after he'd be done from his second job at stables.

He went with his uncle to the seaport where he had a small office, and on their way to there his uncle bought two grilled potatoes filled with cheese and beef. He told Arthur that he was expecting some guests who would arrive at any moment, that's why he chose his office to talk. They sat and they started to have a conversation about the trip. Arthur insisted on going with his friends and asked his uncle to help him make his mother accept to let him go with his friends.

"Rubia, you say?" his uncle said and continued to eat.

"Yes."

He continued to chew the food and think for a bit before giving a response.

"You know, you can go to Serina or any other place like the capital Vetroy, but Rubia... No. And why you're very insistent on going? Just for your friends or for another reason? Tell me the truth."

Arthur looked down at the ground while thinking of what to say.

"You remember the rumors that had been told about your father, don't you? I don't see the point of going there while you know the truth. Your father isn't there."

"Uncle, I know the truth and I trust my father by heart. But my mind cannot go silent and it demands proof and answers. I know the truth as well as I know this sun that is clear up in the sky but I remember you once said 'travelers and wanderers, they don't sail the seas for fun, they have their own reasons and goals to search and achieve!' So, let me think that I have an aim and a reason for my trip." Arthur continued to say, "Maybe, I'd find something about my father. It doesn't have to deal exactly with what people had said before. Maybe, I'd find some trails or a hope."

"You have started to talk like a man, Arthur. Years must have passed quickly and I realized it just now." He nodded his head and continued to say, "I'll speak with your mother this afternoon but know this, I'll not tell her you're going to Rubia. There is no way she'd accept it. Instead, I'll tell her you're going to Serina with your friends. Let's keep this little lie between us, okay?"

"Okay, thank you, Uncle."

"Now, eat the potato before you go to Jones's stable. You spoke and your food got cold."

"Yes... and thank you again, Uncle."

"Mhm."

Shortly after, the guests that his uncle was expecting to come had arrived and Arthur took his leave to Mr. Jones's stable to work.

Arthur started cleaning the stables at Jones's. Mr. Jones had five horses. He used to ride one of them. Now, that horse had become old. It was his favorite because his father gave it to him as a present. The other four horses were mostly used for riding their carriages for his family if they wished to visit relatives or to go to the shops in the capital. Even for nearer shops, they wouldn't go by foot. And sometimes Mr. Jones's daughter would pick one of the four horses to ride for fun. It was a hobby for her.

On this cozy afternoon, too, Miss Jones felt like going on a ride.

"Arthur, prepare one of the horses. I'd like to ride now," Ms. Jones ordered.

"Yes, Miss. Right away," Arthur responded.

Arthur prepared a horse for her and he brought a wooden box for her in order to let her get up on the horse easily. Arthur stood at the front and held the bridle. Once she got up on the horse and took control of it, he let go the bridle.

He stood back and thought to himself, *I know I am just a worker at their stables but it upsets me sometimes the way Ms.*

Jones speaks to me without any respect. I am older than her, yet she calls me by my first name and with commands.

As she was riding the horse, Mr. Jones came out to watch his daughter and it was Arthur's chance to ask him about taking two days off.

Arthur talked with him about it and he accepted but on the condition to work on the weekend too without a bonus. Arthur couldn't negotiate and just accepted.

Once Ms. Jones finished her ride, Arthur took the horse back and fed them. It was already getting dark outside. Arthur went quickly to see Peter in the tannery and asked him if his father had accepted to give them two days off and he told him that he actually did. Arthur cheered up; it was his first time going somewhere out of this town. His heart was happy like a bird, learning to fly for the first time but his happiness wasn't full-filled as he remembered his mother… Arthur hoped that his uncle had talked to her and convinced her.

Arthur arrived home after a long day. "Mother, I'm home," he said as he entered.

His mother was sitting on the chair at the dining table but she said nothing and she refused to look at him.

"Are you well, Mother?" Arthur got worried.

She nodded her head and said, "Go take your bath."

Arthur sniffed himself, *Eww, I smell so bad. Did I smell like this the whole day?*

Arthur usually would go home after he'd finish his job at tannery and take bath and have lunch, and also would take another bath after coming from stable. However, today, he didn't come back home after he finished his job at the tannery.

"I will take a bath right away but…"

"Also, you could have stopped by and told me that you wouldn't be able to come for lunch. I waited for you."

"I am really sorry, Mother. I went out with Peter and Robert to see Billy. He just got back in town. And yes, you're totally right. I should have come here and let you know. I apologize."

"Please don't leave me hanging. I do get worried. You're my only son."

"I won't do it again, I promise."

His mother nodded her head.

"Mother, did my uncle come here?"

"Yes."

"What did he say?"

She looked at Arthur and said, "Arthur, you used to always come to me and talk about everything. Now, you can't? Do you think I'd say no?"

"I'm sorry… I just…I—"

"Now, tell me what did you want to tell me that you couldn't tell it yourself and let your uncle say it instead?"

"I… I don't know from where to start."

"Be straightforward and get to the topic."

"My friends are going for a trip to… to… Serina. Do you mind if I go with them?"

She stood up and looked at him.

"No, I don't mind. Isn't that easy to ask?" She continued to say, "Go with them and have fun. May God protect you."

"Really, Mother?" Arthur's heart finally flew like a bird with happiness and rushed to hug his mother.

She backed off and waved with both of her hands. "No, no, go take a bath first."

Arthur laughed and said, "Can I kiss your cheek at least? Real quick."

"Argh, fine."

Arthur kissed her cheek and she smiled widely. He happily smiled back her too.

3- Arthur's First Voyage

Everything was well prepared. Clothes in bag and well-folded. Arthur made it on time to have a peaceful breakfast and enjoyed it to the last bite. Arthur felt proud of himself to be this well-organized for his first trip. He just had to pick up his bag from his room and get moving.

However, Arthur's mother brought his bag for him.

"Are you sure that you took everything you need?"

"Yes, Mother."

She handed him his backpack and he wore it on his left shoulder. It was a little heavier; it wasn't like this some minutes ago. Arthur was confused and looked at his backpack, it looked like it had got a fat belly. His mother noticed his reaction.

"Oh son, I put some food inside your bag. Just some nuts and dried fruits and yes, a half loaf of bread."

"Oh, I don't need food, there's food there."

"No, you can eat that on your way. I don't know how long it takes to arrive to Serina but normally people would get hungry whenever they travel even if it doesn't take long."

"Right, thank you, Mother."

He hugged his mother; she hugged him tightly and rubbed his back.

"Look after yourself," she said.

"I will. I will."

Then, they looked at each other and smiled. Arthur got this strange feeling or little anxiety for his first voyage. He started to overthink, *I don't know why it feels like I am saying goodbye forever to her and I know I will only be gone for two days. Does this mean I won't come back? Something's going to happen?* Those thoughts took him out of this earth for some moments.

"Arthur?"

He heard his name and he was brought back to reality. "Yes?!"

"One more thing… I want you to get me Serinan spices, hmm, what was it called? Right, I want you to get me Rhus spice."

"Rhus?"

"Yes, Rhus is very common and only found in Serina. It looks too red and it has a little sour taste. I'd like you to get me some of it. It goes well with salad."

"Okay… I will," he said and then thought to himself, *What if I don't find this spice in Rubia?* He looked a little worried.

"And before I forget, I put a small jar and I covered it with a piece of cloth, it has crushed ginger and some honey with it. Take some of it if you feel dizzy or sick while you're sailing the sea."

"Thank you."

Someone knocked on the door. *It must be Peter.*

"I think it's time to go now."

"Yes, I will walk you outside," Arthur's mother said.

Arthur opened the door and it was Peter indeed.

"Hey. Let's go, Arthur." Then he saw Arthur's mother was also leaving the house. He took off his hat and looked at the ground. Showing respect.

"Good morning, ma'am."

"Good morning, Peter. You must be in a rush. I will let you both go, please look after each other. You two are not just friends but brothers. Always remember that."

"Yes, ma'am. Will do."

"Bye, may God keep you both safe."

"Bye," Arthur and Peter replied.

Once they left, Arthur kept looking back at his mother; watching her standing there. Before they turned to right, he raised his hand and waved at her. She waved back to him.

Robert and Billy were waiting for them by the seaport. Arthur saw his uncle and some other men were checking on a ship that had arrived.

"Good morning, Chief."

"Good morning, Arthur. Ready to go for your first trip?"

"Yes. Uncle, what's going on here?"

"Oh, that. We're doing some inspections. Nothing to worry about it. It's just a part of our job, ya know. Got to keep this place safe in such times like this."

"I got it."

"Yes, no matter how long this stuff take us to do, we'd do it," he was really into the topic. "It is our job. We love this country. Gotta protect it with all our might."

"Yes, right."

"Yes? I think I got you bored too quickly with my talk or perhaps I'm making you late. Alright, you go join your friends," he pushed him, "they already got into the ship."

"No, you didn't bore me at all! And yes – I have to go, sorry. Bye!" Arthur said.

Arthur's uncle waved goodbye to Arthur and his friends.

Soon enough, the ship sailed away and the sea waves were too strong. Arthur used to watch the ships and boats while standing at the port. He painted them when he was a kid. It was such a dream for him to be on a ship or a boat. But he never knew how it felt to be in one. He didn't know that sometimes the waves could be strong enough to move the ship; right to left, left to right. His breakfast in his stomach moved in the same rhythm. Peter ran to the edge of the ship, and started to vomit. Billy and Robert laughed at Peter for having seasickness while Arthur placed both of hands on his stomach. He was worried to experience the same thing.

Then Arthur remembered that his mother had put a jar of crushed ginger and honey in his bag. He opened his bag and looked at the many things that his mother had put in it. He had to take out a couple of things first to find the jar. He finally took it out and ate a little of it. Arthur offered Peter to eat from it too and he took a spoon of it. Meanwhile, Billy and Robert were having breakfast, as they hadn't eaten at their homes. Peter had kept his arms wrapped around his waist because he had a stomachache but thankfully, he started to feel little better shortly after and took a nap.

Arthur spent a while looking at the gleaming sea but it felt like the time wasn't passing. He walked around. Most of the people who were on the ship were men and also some families who were going on vacation to one of the islands nearby. Most of families who were traveling had chosen Tanty Island, because it was too quiet. It had beautiful nature and it was actually under the rule of Lillianta.

Lots of people went to Serina which was quite near to Tanty, for either study and get higher degrees or to find cure there. They were famous to have well-achieving doctors there. Just like Billy; he went there for his eyes because he couldn't see well. He'd like to be a teacher as well; he might go there to acquire higher education.

However, Rubia was no longer ruled by Lillianta. It used to be but after the Big War, there was a revolution and by that time, the king didn't want to get his men involved in another war. They went through a big loss even though they had victory. So, it was Rubia's chance to win their independence easily. They freed themselves from all the rules and they didn't want any king, or a president, to rule them until this day.

Finally, Arthur went inside where his friends were resting. He lied down but his thoughts kept him awake for a while as they were getting worse.

If I saw my father in Rubia, would I be happy? What if my father was sick in Rubia the whole time? What if he... He tried to avoid his last thought as it was getting darker and he covered his eyes with his arm, forcing himself to sleep.

A loud voice. A man shouting, "Get up, young men. We have arrived. Get up now."

Arthur opened his eyes and slowly his friends woke up too, except for Peter who was still dreaming. Robert tapped Peter on his shoulder and he woke up frightened, he was looking around thinking where he was at. It was a little funny to watch.

They gathered their stuff and got out of the ship quickly, trying to catch any boat there. They yelled, "Hold on. Stop," but the boats sailed away and the sailors didn't want to go back. This place was a stop for people to rest and get on boats. The water was almost shallow as Serina, Tanty and Rubia were connected by the river. There was no way the ships would sail in the river. So, some big or long boats would come and pick up the travelers. However, Arthur and his friends were asleep, and all the boats had left already.

"What are we going to do?" Arthur said with a tone of worry.

"We just wait. Of course, one of the boats would come back," Robert said.

"Look. WAIT! HEY! Our ship is leaving too," Arthur said loudly.

"Calm down. We'll wait, alright! We're not going back," Robert said.

"Chill out, Arthur. There are some boats we could rent and paddle but normally boats come back and pick up the rest of the travelers," Billy said.

"But we're only four. Would they come back to pick up only us?" Peter asked.

"We'll see. We can always paddle. Let's wait and there's this tiny place that serves drinks or food, possibly. Tea, anyone?" Robert said with a comforting voice.

They drank tea and waited. Then, they had lunch and waited some more. Afternoon was near yet no boats could be seen coming back.

"Guess you young men will rent a boat from me. I will be heading home as well," a man said.

"Looks like we got no choice. Prepare your muscles, guys," Robert spoke.

They rented a boat. Billy sat in the front and Arthur sat in the back. Robert and Peter were on the sides, paddling. The man who rented them the boat told them the directions on how to get to Rubia.

"Argh, I am tired. Billy, tell us a story. What else did you do in Serina?" Peter asked.

"Like what?" Billy was wondering.

"Like falling in love?" Peter asked with a smirk on his face.

Billy laughed out loud and said, "No, seriously no."

Arthur noticed Billy's laugh and he guessed that he was only denying. He knew how Billy and his friends reacted when they got nervous. He was a good observer.

"Come on, you stayed a long time there, you didn't see any girl that you liked?" Peter insisted to know.

"No, why are you very into this topic?" Billy said and scratched his head.

This attitude just proved the fact that he was shy and he was lying about it. Arthur thought to add pressure and tease him to spill out about it but he changed his mind quickly, he didn't want to embarrass him. He thought to ask Billy about it privately some other time.

"Are we halfway yet?" Peter asked.

"Maybe. Can you just stop nagging?" Robert said.

"I want to rest. Can we switch roles now?" Peter demanded.

"I don't know how to paddle," Billy spoke.

"Oh yeah? Then it's your turn, guys. Arthur, come take my position and Billy, take Peter's position but be careful, first let me move and Arthur come here slowly. So, nobody falls off," Robert said.

"Okay," Arthur replied.

The boat was shaking horribly as they switched their places. They found themselves pulling each other's shirts to hang on and not fall. The scene from afar would look like they were dancing on the boat but they weren't. They finally made it. Arthur sat on the left side and Robert sat in the back.

"Now, Peter and Billy."

Peter and Billy carefully switched their positions even though for a second, everyone thought they'd fall off. Billy sighed with relief and fixed his glasses on his nose well.

Robert gave them instructions on how to paddle because Arthur and Billy weren't familiar with that.

Billy and Arthur kept paddling until it felt like forever. The only way there seemed to pass time was to talk.

"Billy, tell us something… I can't continue paddling like this. Guys, talk about something," Arthur demanded.

"Gosh, I'm tired to even to speak," Peter said.

"You can never get tired from speaking. You're just lazy," Robert said.

"I am not lazy! I am probably sleepy," Peter said.

"Yes, sleepyhead," Robert teased him.

"Don't call me that. Don't forget that you used to be the one who would fall asleep in class before," Peter replied.

"Yeah, like you never did?" Robert said.

"Quit it, guys! Alright – I got an idea for a game to play," Billy spoke.

"What is it?" Arthur asked.

"I want you guys to use your imagination," Billy said.

"Imagination? Okay… I think I like this already," Peter responded.

"Yes, your imagination. Imagine that you fell off the boat and woke up to find yourself on an island that you never heard of before. What would you do there? How would you behave?" Billy asked.

"Wow, let me think… or no, I want to take my time. Let Arthur start first, I'm sure he's good at this," Peter said.

"Me? Let's see… I actually can't imagine anything as I'm paddling. I'm not good at multitasking," Arthur told them.

"Is this a way of telling us that you want to take a break?" Robert asked.

"Yes, why not?" Arthur said.

"Hell, no. Don't stop. We barely survived when we switched positions. I won't switch again," Peter said.

"Scaredy-cat," Robert teased Peter again.

"Who?" Peter said.

"Nobody," said Robert.

"Alright, alright, let's continue and let me try to imagine… I think I'd try to find a way to go back home or if the place looks interesting; I'd try to discover the place first then go back home," Arthur said.

"Cool, but what would you tell about yourself to the people there? Would you tell them your name? Or would you pretend to be someone else?" Billy asked curiously.

"Pretend to be someone else? Why? No, I'd tell them about myself and my real name," Arthur said.

"Don't you want to be unknown for once? Be truly you and free too?" Billy asked.

"You think I'm not being true to myself?" Arthur asked.

"I mean… Sometimes, life gets us into things we don't want to deal with, they stop us from doing the things we want to do. Don't you want to tell the people that you're a teacher or a fisherman, or a wanderer or whatever you have always wanted to be? Or you want to tell them that you work in stables and a tannery?" Billy said.

"There's nothing wrong about working in tannery," Peter said angrily.

"I am sorry, I didn't mean to offend anyone here. I am just saying, don't you want to pretend to be what you've always dreamed of to be?" Billy asked.

"I think, no… I think I am realistic but if I see that there were kids on that land that don't know how to write, neither read. I will teach them for a while. Like you said, one of the things I wanted to be is a teacher," Arthur said.

"Good thinking to help children. What about you, Robert?" Billy asked.

"I'd tell the people that I was a knight and I got injured… I fell off from a battleship and I got here. I mean, look at me," Robert said while showing them his biceps. "And… hmm, I might keep my name. I like my name, it sounds powerful," Robert said.

"Awesome! And you, Peter?" Billy asked.

"I'd tell the people there that my lover had died and I'm a broken-hearted wanderer that wants to find a new place to have a fresh beginning in life," Peter said.

Robert, Arthur, and Billy burst into laughter.

"Oh wow, we got a romantic guy here," Billy said.

Peter laughed with blushing cheeks and said, "Guys, come on… It is just an imagination."

"That's why you wanted to know if I fell in love but clearly, you're the one who's in love," Billy said.

Peter chuckled and said, "No, no. Not yet. But I'd like to live a love story. I think everyone does, don't you guys?" Peter said.

"Hey look, I can see lights over there. I think we're very close to reaching Rubia," Arthur spoke.

"Yes, let's hurry up. Arthur, let me paddle. You're not fast," Robert complained.

They switched positions one more time. Robert and Billy continued paddling the rest of the way. And they finally arrived.

Arthur's legs felt numb and he could hardly walk once he got off the boat. It felt as if he had forgotten how to walk.

They collected their stuff with them and decided to look for somewhere to eat and rest. They strolled around the town; it was too loud. The more they walked, the louder the music got and people's singing. People also spoke loudly. Back in their town, it was mostly a quiet place especially in the evening.

It was already dark outside in Rubia but it didn't seem to be dark here. The lights in the streets were too bright, while in Lillianta or actually the village they lived in, Tulipia, the lights were always weak. If Rubia would ever have a different name, Arthur believed people would call it 'Land of Lights', or at least he would.

Arthur and his friends were hungry so they just kept looking for a good place. Many restaurants were open but they couldn't choose which one was best for them. They got tired and stopped in front this place that had a menu written on a board of their food and drinks.

"Let's go in," Robert said. It seemed like Robert knew this place from before.

They all agreed and a man got out of the restaurant; holding a bottle and he burped once and… then twice. He hit his shoulder against the walls, having difficulty in walking.

"Is this a restaurant? You really want to eat from here?" Arthur asked.

"Look up, the sign says 'Restaurant, Bar, and Inn,'" Peter said.

"Let's just find a restaurant with no bar. I don't know how to deal with drunk people," Arthur said with a worried voice.

"I'm not going to walk farther than this, I'm tired. Let's just eat here and also just stay the night if they have rooms available," Peter said.

"I agree, let's eat here and then get some rest," Robert said.

"What you say?" Arthur asked Billy.

"We can go in and eat. We're here together, don't worry," Billy told Arthur.

"Alright then," Arthur said.

They entered inside. Arthur sniffed a disgusting smell… It was stinky; it could be a smell of sweat or could be urine, he wasn't sure. The place looked clean or at least the tables were. And two men were smoking inside but it seemed like nobody was bothered from it.

"Don't you guys want to see another place?" Arthur asked.

A woman came up to them and said, "Welcome, have a seat, gentlemen. We treat our guests like friends."

Arthur felt ashamed because he thought that the woman might have heard what he just said.

She led them to an empty table that had four chairs, and she brought them four jugs of drinks that smelled and looked strange.

"No, thank you," Arthur said.

"No, no, sir. Please, they're for free," she said.

"I don't drink this type of beverage, sorry," Arthur apologized.

"Do you want me to bring you another type of drink? What do you desire?" she asked.

Arthur didn't know what to tell her. He had never heard about those beverages on the menu before.

"Water? Water, will do," Arthur said.

"I'll let you think. I will come back to take your orders once you call me."

Robert grabbed the drink and said, "I'd not say no to a free drink." With a smirk on his face, he drank it up, chugging it all at once. "Ahh, this is good!" It looked like Robert came all the way here to drink.

"Is it… Is it really good?" Peter asked Robert.

"I feel great, man. This is manhood. Drink it up, a man needs to take break and feel great once in a while. Don't be coward to try it. You're a man, you know what you want. And guess what? We're on the land of no rules," Robert said and chuckled.

Arthur wanted to stop Peter but he didn't know how to. Peter, with hesitation, took a huge sip of the drink.

Arthur just hoped that Peter wouldn't like it, so he'd not end up being drunk.

"Garrh, this is strong!" he wiped his mouth with his arm. "Not best of a taste but it gives a feeling of comfort or am I imagining it? I mean, I might be just thirsty," Peter said.

"Man, just enjoy it," Robert said.

"Argh, the aftertaste. This isn't for me, I guess," Peter said.

"Oh, come on, man. Maybe you should try this drink," Robert pointed at one on the menu, trying to convince him.

Arthur looked at Billy and his face was full of hesitation and worries.

"Peter… Robert… Guys, I don't know if this is right."

"Arthur, you are on the land of no rules. Land of freedom. Relax. For how long you're going to follow rules like a kid? Drink it. It is refreshing. I came all the way here to drink this. Gotta refresh my mind, you know."

"No, I don't want to. Just because I stepped on a land that has no rules doesn't mean I should just do whatever. Drinking alcohol is bad and if it would ever be allowed in Lillianta, I'd not drink it." Arthur continued to say, "I thought we came here to discover the place and have a good time."

"This is a fun time," Robert said.

"Arthur is right. Shall we just leave? If the lady has a problem, we can pay for the drinks you just drank if she would charge money for them," Billy said.

"Nope, you can give us your drinks if you guys won't drink," Robert said.

"No. Hey!" Arthur tried to say something while Robert wrapped his arms around the jugs and pulled them toward himself. "You shouldn't drink too much of it…" Arthur said.

"Why do you care? You're not my father," Robert said and drank from Arthur's jug.

"After all, maybe this can calm the pain that is in my heart. I don't get it, why it had to be my father who died and not someone else," Robert said while looking at Arthur. His eyes were full of tears yet they didn't fall on his cheeks. And he drank up.

"So, gentlemen… Are you ready to order food?" the woman asked and told them what was in the menu if they weren't familiar of the name of the meals.

Arthur and Billy decided to order food but take it with them while Peter and Robert stayed to eat. Arthur spoke to Peter aside and told him not to drink too much, so he'd look after Robert as he didn't seem to be alright. Peter promised to stay sober and look after Robert.

They ordered half a loaf of bread filled with black beans that was cooked with tomato sauce for each of them. Once their order was ready, they paid, took the food and left but Arthur's mind stayed there. Worrying about Robert and Peter. Even though they were all adults, but he thought to himself, *As we are together in this trip, we should stick together. I don't understand how this turned out. This is just the beginning of being here. I can't believe that Robert came here and dragged us with him on this trip just… to drink.*

Billy and Arthur sat down on a step of stairs and started to eat their food. While they were eating, Arthur remembered something he read in his father's journal regarding drinking alcohol. One day, a man offered him a drink and Arthur's father kindly refused it. The man kept insisting to make him drink and he told him, "A true man doesn't drink to hide his issues neither to numb his sorrow. A true man doesn't drink to have fun; he doesn't need a drink for that. You can find joy as you're sober. You can deal with life's difficulties as you're sober because your mind can think better and always better when you're wide awake. Solutions don't come up when your mind is in a haze. I believe that alcohol is more useful for medicine, such as to clean wounds. Why would I drink something that cleans wounds?"

There was time when Lillianta allowed alcoholic drinks but people complained, especially women. They suffered from their drunk husbands. The shops owners couldn't handle drunk people smashing the windows of their shops. Once the order came to prohibit alcoholic drinks, families finally started to find peace.

Rubia might be the land of freedom but not many people were happy. Many of them moved to neighboring countries, especially families who were worried for their children to turn bad. Maybe, people didn't like rules but some rules were actually meant for their good.

"You liked the meal?" Billy asked and Arthur was brought out of his thinking bubble.

"Yes, it tasted good," Arthur said.

"I like the taste of parsley," Billy commented.

"Yes, indeed," Arthur agreed.

"So, where are we going to stay for the night?" Billy wondered.

"I don't know. We can keep looking, if you want to?" Arthur said.

"I am tired, Arthur. What about the boat? We're not far away to it," Billy suggested.

"Is it safe to sleep outdoors here?" Arthur was worried again.

"I don't know. Let's go and see. I think people are just busy in the restaurants and bars," Billy responded.

They walked a little bit farther and they saw nobody was around the boats. So, the boat would serve as their accommodation for the night. It was small but it fit them well.

They lay down in opposite directions. Billy's feet would meet Arthur's head. Arthur's feet would meet Billy's head.

Arthur stayed up watching the sky. He couldn't see the stars. *I think the stars don't like to have a competitor that shines against them. The lights of the town might have bothered the stars and they decided to fade away and settle upon another town. Empty skies make me sleepless.*

"Billy, did you fall asleep?"

"Mhm."

"That means you're not asleep."

"Arthur, just close your eyes and you'll sleep."

"I tried but I couldn't."

"I'm sure you didn't close them properly. I know you like to observe everything around you. Just close your eyes and…"

"And what?"

"Goodnight!"

Arthur sighed. "Goodnight, Billy."

He didn't close his eyes; he just sat up and looked at the river. The lights were amazingly reflected on the water, just like a black mirror. He tried to capture this view so well in his memory, so he could paint it once he'd be back home.

Suddenly, he heard footsteps. He looked around and he saw a man. The man saw Arthur and he took off his hat to greet him and wore it once again. Arthur nodded his head and stood up.

"Are you a wanderer?" the man asked.

"No… I'm here for a vacation with my friends. What about you, sir?"

"Well, I'm a merchant. I buy perfumes, spices, and clothes and resell them in different cities and countries."

"Mhm."

"I actually saw you earlier in the restaurant. I didn't know I'd see you here as well."

Did he follow me all the way? Is he a thief or what is on his mind? Arthur looked at Billy, he was fast asleep.

"What a coincidence," Arthur responded.

"You're a real gentleman, you and your friend; you two held on your own values too tight while you're only too young," he complimented.

"What do you mean? Which values?"

"Not to drink alcohol."

"Ah, right. I see."

I wonder what he wants to tell me now, Arthur wondered.

"Alright, then. This is where I will sleep tonight." He pointed at a boat on the right. "Being a merchant isn't easy, sometimes. My cousin and his friend, we would shift through the nights to look after our goods. Tonight, it is my turn to sleep in the boat."

"I understand, and it is getting late too already."

"Yes, I hope you enjoy your stay. Goodnight."

"Goodnight, sir," he took off his hat while he walked away to his boat.

Suddenly, Arthur got this idea in his mind. He knew he shouldn't trust a stranger but he couldn't think wisely enough at this very moment. He thought that since this man was a merchant and would have traveled to many places, there was a chance he might have seen his father.

"Sir… Can I ask you a question?"

He stopped and turned to look back at Arthur. "Yes?"

"I want to show you something…"

Arthur opened his backpack and again he had to take some of the things out of his bag, and Arthur felt embarrassed of how many things he took out, to reach his father's portrait. He left his bag and the things he took out on the boat. He held and looked at the portrait with sparkling eyes. It was a white and black photograph, he wished his father's portrait was in colors but all the portraits were still in black and white at that time. In this portrait, his father looked young but he hoped this gentleman would recognize him.

Arthur went to the merchant and showed it to him.

"Do you know this gentleman, sir?"

"I might have seen him before but I can't remember when or where exactly."

"Can you try to remember when and where? Please try, sir," Arthur insisted.

He sighed and said, "I'd be guessing that I had seen him some years ago, maybe 8 years ago or more than that. Is he a merchant or a fisherman?"

"A fisherman."

"I don't think I have seen him recently. It could be way back in time."

"You didn't see him in Rubia?"

"No, I don't think so. Probably in Lillianta. Why are you asking?"

"My father has been missing for 10 years, since he sailed with a group of fishermen to the ocean."

"Oh, I'm sorry son. What makes you think that he's in Rubia?"

"Some people said that they saw him here."

"I don't think that he's here. I come here often." He continued to say, "Many men were lost once they reached the ocean, I heard it too. They could be found on a no-man's land or somewhere in the far west or..." he said and paused.

"Or?"

"Maybe the ocean monster showed up to him that day," he spoke in very quiet voice.

"Do you believe that there's an ocean's monster?"

"Shhh... Young man, don't talk about ocean's monster loudly. It could be just a tale but nobody would dare to speak about it." He continued to say, "Yes, I do. Did your father do justice in his life? Was he faithful in his job and with family and friends?"

"Yes."

"Did he have an extreme pride?"

"No, he was humble."

"He's going to be fine, I hope. Ocean's monster mostly swallows unjust men and who have extreme pride and it'd throw them back up after days or years... Then people would find them on a seashore one day but dead. That's what I heard. It could be only a myth."

Arthur remained silent for a bit. *My father wasn't found on the seashore among the dead. Does this mean he's alive somewhere else far west? Is he living alone on an empty island?*

The merchant looked at how Arthur's face turned into a frown quickly. "I'm sorry to mention this to you."

"Sir, does the monster do justice?" Arthur asked.

The man shrugged while holding his hat in his hand and said, "It's a monster, what can you expect from a monster? Isn't it meant to be cruel? However, God knows justice. He could have kept him safe somewhere. Anyways, young man, it's time for me to go and sleep. Goodnight and yeah, if you want to ask someone about your father in here. Ask the chief of Rubia. Well, he's not a chief; he's more likely to be a wise old man. Yet, some people refer to him as a chief." He put his hat on his head again.

"Thank you, sir."

"Goodnight."

"Goodnight," Arthur called after him.

The man went to his boat to sleep. Arthur gathered his stuff, put them back along with the portrait into his bag, and lay down in the boat. He put his bag under his head like a pillow but it was too filled to the maximum and his neck didn't feel comfortable. He moved it off from under his head. He sighed and he finally closed his eyes and allowed himself to try to sleep.

4- The Heart Knows the Truth

The sun rose for another day yet Arthur was still asleep. The sun tried to wake him up and warmed up his cheeks. He opened his eyes and he covered them with his arm quickly. The sunlight was strong to have his eyes open with ease. Arthur got off the boat and started to crawl towards the river to wash his face and to awaken himself.

"Did you get drunk in your dreams, Arthur? Why you're crawling?"

"I am going to wash my face... Oh Peter, hi!"

"Well, good morning!"

"Yeah." Arthur washed his face. "Good morning. How are you?"

"I'm good, just having a headache and a stomachache. Listen, I don't like this trip so far."

"Oh, come on. Don't say that. Our trip has just started. Let's go and explore the place. Where's Robert?" Arthur looked around and didn't see Billy. "And Billy?"

"Robert is sleeping. I don't think he'd wake up any sooner. He went mad last night."

"What happened?"

"After he drank, he went into three stages. At first, he was angry... Too angry, then in the second stage he started to cry for a while. I didn't know what to do. He drank more and the third stage came; he started to sing and dance with old women and men. It was crazy, true madness. He danced for too long, I didn't know from where he got this energy. But put that all aside, there's something important I need to tell you."

"What's it?"

"Robert isn't okay. He's angry at you. He's holding so much of anger against you."

"What? Don't be silly. You're joking, right?"

"No," Peter looked serious.

Peter noticed Billy was coming toward them. "I will talk to you about it later."

"Hi again, Peter. Good morning, Arthur," Billy said while holding a paper bag filled with food.

Peter nodded his head.

"Good morning, Billy. Where did you go?"

"Look at this, I went to bring food for all of us. Where's Robert? He didn't wake up yet?"

"Not yet," Peter said.

"Well, we can eat and save some for him," Billy said.

They sat together and had breakfast. Billy told his friends what he saw earlier; he saw little shops in the middle of the town which were covered under shades. He recommended them to come with him to see them. Peter wasn't into it. He felt sick from yesterday and he'd just continue resting until early afternoon to go back home.

"At 1 o'clock. Let's meet here and leave," Peter said.

Billy looked at his pocket watch. "We still have four hours. That's not bad."

"Peter if you start to feel better, come join us. We'd be in the shops that Billy described and maybe swim. What do you think, guys?" Arthur suggested.

"No… I don't think so," Peter didn't agree.

"We can just shop and discover the place," Billy wasn't into the idea either.

Arthur sighed "It's sunny though but alright. No pressure."

"Arthur, do you still have ginger and honey?" Peter asked.

"Yes, I do." Arthur took it out from his bag. "Here, you can keep it with you."

"Thank you," Peter said and ate from it. "You don't know, this thing is magical."

"You're welcome. My mother gave it to me."

"I'll make sure to thank her once we're back."

Once they were done eating, Peter asked Arthur to talk aside alone and he told him to be careful when he's around Robert and not to argue back with him. Arthur didn't take it seriously, he thought it was a joke but Peter said something that made Arthur be concerned. "Last night, Robert said, 'Arthur's father could be still alive and my father is dead. My father kept fighting with Arthur's father, trying to prove who's better at fishing each time and Arthur's father would win. And he also won at this. I don't know but life is unfair.'" Peter continued to say, "But listen, Arthur, don't worry much about it. People when they grieve, they do go through stages too… One of them is to blame themselves or other people. It shall take time but please stay away from him for a while."

Arthur nodded his head. He was unhappy to hear this. He had been thinking that this trip would help Robert and he would have a great time with them. He didn't expect it to take this bad turn.

"Go to Billy, he's waiting. I will get some rest."

"Alright, take care."

"Sure."

Arthur joined Billy and they were ready to explore the place. Rubia was too quiet in the morning. The town looked empty and most of the stores were closed. It was surprising, compared to how it was during the evening. Lillianta would be way energetic in the morning.

As they got closer to the center of the town where the small shops were at, Arthur immediately changed his mind of what he thought earlier. It was too loud and full of energy again. People were selling clothes, shoes, rugs, and carpets. They walked further and found people selling vegetables and fruit. The fruit were too shiny; Arthur liked how they made sure to clean each single fruit but didn't like the fact that it actually made him crave to get some and at the same time he felt still full from breakfast. *It's just so unfair,* he thought.

They reached the shops that were selling perfumes and on the other side people were selling spices. *Oh yes, spices! My mother told me to buy her... I forgot its name.*

"Hey, Billy, do you know a type of spice that is red in color?"

"Paprika?"

"No... It's well-known in Serina and they mostly use it for salad."

"Ah, Rhus you mean?"

"Yes! Help me to look for it. If you see it anywhere here, tell me."

"All right; however, I don't think they sell it here."

"Please let's search for it, maybe we'd find some."

"All right."

They looked and asked at each shop. Until they realized, they had failed and found nothing. Now, Arthur started to be seriously worried about it. *My mother would find out about where I was… She'd be quite upset with me. I don't want her to be sad and angry. Maybe I'd lie to her that I forgot to buy it but for how long would I keep lying?* Arthur sighed. *I am just hopeless.*

"We have some time left. Do you want to continue discovering the place or go back and re-join the guys?"

"We can go back… No wait, I need to talk to someone here."

"Who?"

"The chief of Rubia."

"Why?"

"I want to ask him about my father."

"Oh… I see. Let's ask this man, he looks to be a local man. He must know where the chief stays."

They asked the man and he told them that the chief's house wasn't far from here. His house was painted in light blue. It was the only house that was colored in blue in that neighborhood and it was mostly covered with plants.

Soon enough, they found the house with the same description. Arthur got too nervous about knocking on the door but he collected his strength. *I have to do this,* he thought. He knocked on the door and Arthur felt as if his heart was the one that got knocked on.

"The door is open," came a voice of an old man.

"Go, enter," Billy said.

"Aren't you coming with me?" Arthur asked.

"You want to speak with him about your father, it must be personal," Billy said.

"It's okay, please come with me," Arthur insisted.

"Okay," Billy said.

They entered his house, and the house was pretty small. Arthur saw the old wise man was sitting on the floor on a mat and in front of him was a short table where he had papers and books. He had tons of books; the books were everywhere, from corner to corner. Behind him, there was a bed. The whole house was just a single room which was filled with books and a single bed.

"How can I help you young men?" the old man asked.

His voice sounded really deep and it reminded Arthur of his late grandfather's voice. It brought him some sort of comfort but he was still a little nervous and nearly forgetting the words that he wanted to say.

Billy gently pushed Arthur's back. "Come on, speak."

Arthur nodded his head and cleared his throat.

"Sir, I… I come here to ask you…"

"Yes?" he said and he wore his glasses. Arthur was thinking about the fact that Billy wasn't the only one now who was wearing those. He quickly shook the thought.

"I… I'd like to ask you if you… if you know someone called Edward Byron."

"Edward Byron? Edward Byron? Hm, I'm afraid, I have not."

Arthur took off his backpack from his shoulders and he tried his best to pull his father's portrait out of his bag without having other things fall out. He walked toward him and showed it to him.

"This is him. Did you see him before?"

"This man… Yes, he's a fisherman. I remember him. I used to buy fish from him long, long time ago. He was always honest and always brought fresh big fish with fair prices. But I don't know why he doesn't come here to sell fish by the port anymore."

"Yes. May I ask when was the last time you saw him?"

"Oh son, that must have been ages. I could only remember him because of his fair prices."

"Oh, okay." Arthur sighed and took back the portrait and put it into his bag.

"Is there something wrong?"

"My father went missing ten years ago… In the ocean."

"I see. I see. If it has been 10 years and you heard nothing bad happened to him, then there's hope, son. He could be still alive somewhere."

"How do you know?"

"The ocean… isn't quite safe. However, your father looked like a good gentleman. You know, when you do good in life, you receive good in return. When you do bad, bad things will happen to you. So, he's a good man like I said. He should be fine. Maybe he's trying to come back but couldn't yet. Who knows?"

"That's right. Thank you," Arthur said with deep relief.

"No problem. Anything else, gentlemen?"

"No, thank you."

"All good then."

"Goodbye!" Arthur and Billy were ready to leave.

"Gentlemen?" the old chief called.

"Yes?" Arthur and Billy responded at same time, and they turned around to look at him.

"Before you leave, I'd like to tell you this. You two, if you keep being the way you're now, you'll have a promising future," he said.

"Thank you," Arthur and Billy said.

"Especially you," he pointed at Arthur.

"Me?" Arthur asked, full of surprise.

"Yes," he paused then said, "and your friend is a true friend because he didn't react badly or jealously when I pointed at you only. He's not an envious person at all, he's happy for you."

Arthur smiled widely and he placed his hand on Billy's shoulder.

"He's indeed a great friend."

Billy kept smiling at Arthur and at the wise man.

"God bless you two and may you have a safe journey back to your home," he finally said.

"Thank you."

"Thank you!"

And they left.

Arthur found the conversation with the wise man quite interesting. He wished to have his wisdom one day. He found comfort in his words and he was overwhelmed. *I don't know how he could know about us this fast and even saying we'd have a promising future. I believe he's good in analyzing personalities. I don't think he can predict the future, or can he? No, I don't believe in such things.* Arthur shook his head.

"What's wrong? You have been shaking your head too often lately," Billy asked.

"Oh, did I? I'm just overthinking sometimes," Arthur said.

"Mhmm."

"Hey, Billy?"

"Yes?"

"I wanted to ask you this since yesterday but as we're alone now, I'd like to ask you… Who is she?"

"Who? What do you mean?"

"The girl you like in Serina."

"Oh gosh, you got me, huh?" Billy laughed.

"I know how you guys behave when you get nervous or lie about something."

"You surely do, you observe as much as I do, too. Don't forget that, I know your attitude too."

Arthur laughed. "I know… I know but you know it's not me who's hiding a love story now."

Billy laughed out loud nervously.

They continued to walk and Billy didn't add anything to the conversation. Arthur decided not to push him to talk about it. He preferred that Billy would speak by himself without pressure further.

Before they arrived to the river side, Billy stopped and Arthur wondered why he had stopped now. Billy finally confessed.

"She works in the clinic where I had my eyes checked up. She still studies too. She's an amazing person but she's too young."

"How young?"

"Two years younger."

"Are you for real? Two years are nothing."

"I know but I sometimes think that younger girls don't think the way I do."

"I don't think so. Girls mostly become mature in mind before boys."

"Yes, but I'm different. I'm an old soul, you know that, bud."

"I know. But… If you like her, then doesn't it mean you are both at same level of thinking?"

"Almost."

"Almost? Well, almost is a good sign to be the same."

Billy chuckled and said, "You're right. I know you're not going to tell anyone but I want to emphasize this, please don't tell the guys. They won't stop laughing at me."

"Don't worry. I won't reveal anything to them until you find the right time to tell them. And hey! Don't hold the wedding in Serina away from us. I want to see you dancing the Lilliantian traditional dance," Arthur said and laughed.

Billy laughed too.

"If I get married in Serina, I'd not have to dance the Lilliantian dance there, right? Maybe I should consider about holding the wedding there indeed."

"No, come on, buddy, don't say that."

Billy chuckled. "I am just joking."

They arrived at the riverside and they saw Robert there and Peter. Arthur waved at them.

"Why were you smiling? Or even laughing about?" Robert asked and he looked to be not in a great mood.

"The day looks sunny and beautiful. That's a good reason to smile," Arthur said.

"Are you becoming a poet now Mr. Byron?" Robert asked.

"No… Well, how are you today?" Arthur asked with concern.

"What do you mean with 'today'? I'm alright, okay?" Robert said.

"He means how are you on this fine day?" Billy spoke.

"Billy the Professor has spoken," Robert said.

"Guys, can we just leave now? I don't want to miss the ship," Peter said.

"Neither do we," Billy said.

"Let's go," Robert said.

Everyone put their stuff and got in the boat except for Arthur. He noticed from afar; there was another boat that was about to leave and there was that man whom he talked with last night, the merchant.

"Guys, please wait for me. I will be right back," Arthur said.

He ran toward their boat and he shouted, "Sir? Sir… Can I talk to you for a moment please?"

The man looked at Arthur and he recognized him. He asked the other men to stop and to wait for a little bit.

"How are you, young man? You got good news about your father?" he asked.

"I don't know if it was good." Arthur spoke his mind out loud. "I actually need your help."

"I'll try to help you as long as it's something I can help with," he said.

"Last night, you mentioned that you buy spices and resell them."

"Yes, spices and type of clothes and many other things."

"Yes, do you have Rhus?"

"Of course, I have, but not that much. I'm heading to Serina today to buy more."

"Can I get some, please? I'd like to buy it."

"I don't have a lot and it's not quite fresh, I must tell you."

"It's okay. I'll buy it."

"A small bag of Rhus like this one, I normally sell it for 1 don but since it's not that fresh, I'll sell it to you for half a don. You still want it?"

"Yes, sir." He took out a half don out of his pocket and paid him. The merchant gave him the bag of the spice.

"Thank you, sir."

"No problem. Take care."

Arthur nodded and got back to the boat and put the bag of Rhus into his bag.

"Sorry, guys. Let's go. I'll paddle if you don't mind."

"Of course, we do not mind at all. Go ahead, Mr. Bryon," Robert said.

Peter and Arthur paddled half of the way. Then it was Billy and Robert's turn to paddle the rest of the way. They tried to talk to ease the way back and make it feel shorter. However, oddly Robert didn't speak that much with them. Arthur thought that when they'd travel to Rubia, Robert would have a change of atmosphere and he might feel better, while in fact he had gotten way worse now.

They made it on time to the seaport and paid the rest of the money to the man who had rented them the boat. They ran to catch up with the ship which was getting ready to sail away to Lillianta.

The trip going back to Lillianta felt shorter. Perhaps, it felt this way because they were going home and it's always great to be home again. It's true Arthur was away for almost two days and it was a short voyage but he surely missed his mother so much. He couldn't wait to see her and tell her all about the trip and how useful that ginger and honey was.

Again, the guys were sleeping and Arthur stayed awake. He didn't want to miss a single detail of the sunset and how fast it got dark for evening to start. They were near to their homeland. Arthur liked to look at the dark waves of the sea. Most of people didn't like to look at the sea at night. They found it terrifying but not for Arthur, because he believed it's not as dark as it looked like. This could be a sign for him to be sailor, a wanderer of the sea.

Arthur could see Lillianta's seaport and he could see a woman was standing beside a big streetlamp there. She was wearing a pale orange scarf loosely and a beautiful brown dress and as usual, she was wearing old leathered shoes that Arthur had always wanted to fix but she always refused to let him repair them for her. She smiled and her eyes teared a little bit as she saw him waving at her. She was his dear mother. Arthur remembered he used to wait for his father with her at the port for him to come back and Arthur had never imagined that his mother would stand there to wait for his return from a trip one day.

"Guys, we have arrived. Wake up... Robert, Peter, Billy... Come on, wake up!"

They slowly woke up. "Guys, I'll leave now. My mother is waiting for me at the port. I will go to see her. Open your eyes wide and get up, okay?"

He grabbed his backpack and left quickly. Once he reached her, he stood before her; she held his head and kissed his forehead.

"I want to hug you but I'm afraid you'd feel embarrassed as your friends are here," his mother said.

"Nah, I'd not be ashamed," he wrapped himself around her.

Maybe some would make fun of me for being naive. Yet, in this moment, I don't care. Moments like this are to be treasured and I will never say no when it is an embrace that comes from my mother, he thought.

"Goodnight, Mrs. Byron; goodnight, Arthur," Billy said as he passed by.

"Goodnight Billy," Arthur and his mother said.

"Goodnight," Robert said.

Arthur nodded and said, "Goodnight, buddy."

"Mrs. Byron, Mrs. Byron, the crushed ginger with honey really saved my life. Thank you, ma'am," Peter said.

Arthur's mother smiled at him and said, "I'm glad that it helped you. I hope you're feeling well now."

"I am. Thank you. Goodnight, ma'am. See you tomorrow, Arthur."

"See you."

"Goodnight, Peter," Arthur's mother said.

As they're about to leave, Arthur saw his uncle was leaving his office, yawning. He was going to check and inspect the ship. This was the last ship that they were expecting. Thank God they were able to get on it before it was too late. They greeted him and said goodnight.

On their way home, Arthur told his mother a little bit about the trip. Arthur couldn't tell her a lot because he was afraid to say 'Rubia' instead of 'Serina'. He stammered a few times. He was not sure for how long he would be able to keep up with this lie and he never liked to lie and he was never good at it. He just hoped she'd forget about the trip eventually and soon.

They arrived home then and there were two things on Arthur's mind; a warm bath and going to bed to sleep. But before all that, he decided to give his mother the spice that she asked for. He put his backpack on his bed and he took out the spice. He went to his mother and showed it to her.

"Oh, thank you, dear. I was afraid that you might forget to buy me this."

"You're welcome."

His mother's face was too empty and he felt there was something wrong.

"Arthur, please have a seat."

Yes, there's something wrong. He pulled the chair and sat down.

"You brought me the spice. It's true, my mind is convinced now, but my heart isn't. Tell me, where did you go to? Was it Rubia?"

Arthur was shocked and wondered how she knew about it. He said nothing and avoided eye contact with her.

"Son. My heart knows your eyes too well. I know when you lie or when you tell the truth. I think you can lie to anyone on this earth but not to me." His mother continued to say, "I know you want to see things yourself to make sure but wasn't it enough to follow your heart? Don't you trust your father?"

"Mother… I trust him by heart but… I don't know, I wanted to go and ask… Mother, forgive me for lying to you. Please forgive me." He held her hand.

She pulled him into a hug.

"It's okay. I'll understand your situation this time but please don't do it again."

He let go and said, "I won't do it again. I promise." He looked at her in the eye.

"Good." She let go a sigh of relief then said, "You must be hungry, let me serve dinner."

"Oh, is it okay if I go and take a bath first?"

"Yes, I will reheat the food meanwhile."

He nodded his head and went to the bathroom. While he was taking a bath, his mind was wildly regretting what he had done. *I don't understand my mind sometimes. It pushes me to do things unwisely.* He sighed. *At least my mother has forgiven me… I know she's a very kind-hearted woman but I shouldn't have used her kindness in a situation like this. I won't lie, neither hide anything from her again.*

Arthur rested his head back and looked at the ceiling. *Gosh, tomorrow I'll have to go to work again, I think I have enjoyed travelling more than my daily life. I wonder when my next trip would be. I hope it's going to be soon.*

5- *Maxemus* the Warrior Is Ready

Autumn was quick and winter had started in the blink of an eye. It was too cold when it snowed. Lilliantian people hadn't witnessed snow for over five years. It was incredible and magical. Everyone was happy to see the snow again and the kids; oh wow, they had started a snowballs war. They literally made two trenches in the snow on two sides, and they would hide in them. Once one of them yelled, "War," and everyone started to throw snowballs at each other. Arthur, Billy, and Peter were jealous for not thinking of this game before to play when they were kids. But that didn't stop them. They threw snowballs at each other too.

Robert kept travelling and when he'd come back, he wouldn't talk with Arthur and other friends a lot. He only talked to them about the fact that he made a few new friends in Rubia that he'd visit every once in a while, and he'd go to Tanty to visit some of his relatives. Arthur tried to visit him a couple of times before but whenever he'd go to his house, his older brother or his mother would tell him that Robert's not here or was sleeping.

After a while in the winter, it was announced that *Maxemus*, the ocean's fighter, was fully rebuilt and ready to sail. Newspaper announced the news everywhere in Lillianta.

Some people even hung the newspaper on their store door to share the good news with everyone. However, most of the people highly recommended not to sail in the harsh winter. Sailing in the winter could be dangerous. Due to this reason, everyone waited for spring to come. And here it was.

The birds would chirp at Arthur's windows every morning and whenever he'd go to the backyard in the morning, he could smell the wet grass and flowers' perfume in the air clearly. The dewy drops were still on the leaves and some of those drops fell off, like a shy drizzle.

It was Sunday and tomorrow's the day when sailors were finally sailing the ocean. Everyone was going to the great hall in downtown where everyone from different religion would unite in order to pray for better days and pray for the men who would sail the ocean tomorrow.

For this occasion, Arthur was wearing his father's suit. His father was a tall man. Arthur was tall enough yet his father would be still taller than him. Arthur's mother had fixed the shirt, the jacket, and the pants of the suit for Arthur to fit well on him.

Arthur admired the suit and he felt his father was present with him on this day as he was looking at the mirror. He was all ready and couldn't wait to go to the great hall.

"I'm ready. Shall we go, Mother?"

"Wait a moment, son."

She went back to her room to bring the holy book with her. She placed it on the table and went to the kitchen to bring a basket.

"Son, please carry this basket and I'll hold the holy book with me," she said and picked up the holy book from the table.

"Basket?"

Arthur wondered what was inside it and he opened it. He saw fruit and…

His mother hit his hand and the lid of the basket closed itself. He couldn't see the rest.

"When will you stop being curious?" his mother asked.

"I don't know." He rubbed his head awkwardly.

"Let's go now."

They left the house and went on their way to the great hall. People kindly greeted each other. Everyone seemed to be happy today. Even the sun was shining happily up in the sky, lighting up the town with a bright smile. It was just a beautiful day indeed.

Once they had arrived, they saw that many people had already arrived before. There were people who came from other places of Lillianta. They could be recognized easily from the way they were dressed. Their clothes represented where they came from or what religion they believed in. Arthur was excited how the prayers would be like. *It's true we don't share the same religion but surely, we're praying to the same one God,* thought Arthur.

"Arthur, give me the basket. I'll be right back. Don't move from your spot, so I can find you when I'm back. It's crowded already," Arthur's mother said.

"Oh, okay. Here…" he gave her the basket.

Arthur stood there waiting for his mother. People passed by him until one guy bumped into Arthur's shoulder as he walked by him. Arthur rubbed his shoulder because it hurt him a little and he looked back to see who that was. He couldn't recognize him as he walked in a fast pace and carelessly. But he was blond and as tall as Robert. *I don't think it was Robert... I mean, I don't see his family around here yet and why would he bump into me without apologizing? I'm sure he'd apologize to whoever he accidentally bumps into.*

"Arthur?" his mother called him.

He looked in the direction of her voice.

"Come, let's sit over here before the prayers start," his mother said.

He nodded his head in agreement and joined her. They sat together.

Shortly after, everyone started to pray in their own ways. It felt too peaceful and it looked too beautiful to see people gathering for a reason like this. Arthur felt his heart and soul were being filled up with positivity and strong energy.

After they finished the prayer, everyone sat around long tables. There was a feast too and people started to put the food on the table and serve it. *The smell, oh the smell is just wonderful. It smells delicious and I am sure it tastes delicious too,* Arthur thought. There were roasted turkeys and chickens, they had been roasted in wood-fire ovens. There were fruit and salads. *I don't know from where to start. I want to get some of the turkey but it's too far from me. I guess I'll just eat chicken; I haven't eaten chicken in a long time too.*

Arthur served some food for himself and for his mother. He noticed that Billy was sitting at the same table but he was far from them. Arthur nodded his head and smiled at him. Billy did the same in return.

Arthur picked his fork and was just going to dig in, but his mother stopped him.

"Wait, eat salad or fruit first," his mother said.

"But, Mother..."

"But, Arthur, this way is healthier. Trust me."

He did what he was told. He grabbed an apple and cut it into halves. He gave one half to his mother and he ate the other half of the apple. Then finally, he was ready to enjoy his chicken meal with vegetables. "Mmm." *It tastes delicious; just how I expected it to be. I think I can become an expert at this.*

After half an hour, almost everyone was done eating; a huge volunteering group came to take the plates to wash them and they kept the left overs for whoever didn't make it for the gathering. Arthur liked the idea of having people to volunteer, he didn't know about it earlier. *I should have joined them; I guess it's never too late.* He got up and helped carrying the plates with them. He noticed that more people just came and helped too. It brought such good vibes, it felt everyone was one family.

Once the plates were being collected, people began to leave the great hall and Arthur went to the port where *Maxemus* was. It was too crowded there; he could see it from afar because it's huge. It was the biggest ship among the rest. Arthur took his time to just observe it. He saw people go and touch it and would say a prayer again to protect it, some people let float paper lanterns on the water beside *Maxemus* and some let them fly in the air. Arthur had heard about paper lanterns but this was his first time he was seeing them. He was curious if these people would allow him to fly one. He got close to them and stood there hoping someone would notice him.

There was a man who had a couple of paper lanterns and he saw Arthur was standing and looking at the beauty of lanterns. He just smiled at Arthur and looked away.

"Excuse me, sir?" Arthur tried to grab his attention.

The man bowed to him and Arthur felt shy and he bowed too. This was his first time to see a person that greeted him that way.

"Can I try one please?" Arthur asked.

He nodded his head.

"Make a prayer or a wish," he said.

"Can I make both?"

He nodded his head and he handed Arthur the paper lantern and he lighted it up. Arthur was a little surprised to see how big the flame was and he tried to hold it well so it wouldn't slip from his hand and fly way. Arthur managed to hold it well and he closed his eyes.

I pray for; safety, protection, and success for Maxemus *ship. I wish that I'd see my father very soon.* He opened his eyes and he let go of the paper lantern and it flew away... Arthur's eyes were sparkling while watching the lantern and they were sparkling because they were full of tears. Arthur got a little emotional. He put all his energy and thought into this lantern.

"Thank you, sir," Arthur said.

He bowed and Arthur bowed too.

Later on, he saw his mother, and his uncle and his wife were standing right by the corner. Arthur greeted his uncle and wife. His uncle couldn't hold back his excitement and began to explain to them about how *Maxemus* was built and he leaded them to it. They got closer to it and it looked really massive up-close and it looked just the same like in the portrait and paintings that Arthur had seen before in books. *Maxemus* was repaired twice during the past 100 years after the war had ended between a group of countries; Lillianta was one of them that went to fight against Oernatus. *Maxemus* was on its way back to Lillianta after the war against Oernatus ended; however, it started to fall apart and sank into the ocean. Now, it was rebuilt in the same way.

I'd not know if it's a new one because it looks exactly the same!

"Look, sister, it's too strong, it's a warrior," Arthur's uncle said proudly.

"I hope so," Arthur's mother said.

"What do you mean? Come on, look at it, touch it. The material is way too tough; nothing can stand against it." Arthur's uncle knocked on it.

"Hun, don't say that. Let's just hope that everything will be alright," his wife spoke.

"I'd never understand women. You always lay on hopes and wishes, while the truth is real before your eyes. This is the strongest ship we have ever made," he said.

"Yes… Okay, Brother. Now… How about you two come with us to my home? You and Alessia haven't visited me together for a very long time," Arthur's mother requested.

"Yes, right, let's go, Tryess," his wife said.

"But I'm busy," he said.

"Please, at least for a short while. I picked up chamomile that I dried lately, I can make tea out of it and with honey. I also baked some ginger biscuits this morning."

"Tryess! Our baby wants Medlee's ginger cookies, I'm craving it now," his wife said while she caressed her belly.

"Hmm, alright, alright, just for a short while. I need to meet the men and talk to them before the evening so everything will be set and ready," he said.

"Sounds good, shall we go home together now?" Arthur's mother asked.

"Yes," he said.

They all walked together and suddenly a heavy strong arm grabbed Arthur.

"Why, my nephew is way too quiet today?" and he pulled him aside.

"Uncle!" *Argh. That was really out of blue!* Arthur got scared.

"Well, I don't know. I was just listening to you all talking," Arthur spoke.

"Yes, there's nothing wrong about listening too. Are you nervous about going with us tomorrow?"

"I am not. I mean… I'm not going with you tomorrow."

"What? Why not?"

"Because…"

"I got it. I got it. It's your mother. I will talk to her once we arrive to your house, okay?"

"Okay."

He messed Arthur's hair. "Cheer up, young man, and you need a haircut; when the last time you cut it, huh?"

"It's been a while," Arthur said while fixing his messy hair.

They arrived home; everyone managed to sit except for Arthur. He went inside his room to bring a chair to sit with them. His mother picked a good bunch of chamomiles that she had dried yesterday and took it with her to the kitchen to make tea.

"Arthur, please come and help me."

"Yes, Mother."

She gave him two plates of ginger cookies and he served them on the dining table.

Once the chamomile tea was ready, his mother came to serve it to all of them.

Everyone was chilling and talking about several topics until Arthur's uncle brought up about tomorrow's trip. The joy quickly disappeared and the worries had increased.

"Well, Arthur is coming with us, right?" he said.

"No. Don't open this topic now, Brother. He'll stay here. I can't let myself worry about you and my son at same time. I cannot," she said.

"But, Sister, there's nothing to worry about. *Maxemus* is the strongest ship ever and you shouldn't worry about us. We're men and your son is a man now. How old are you, Arthur? 16? 17? 18?"

"17. I will be 18 in the summer," Arthur answered.

"See, he's 17; he is a man, not a child anymore."

"You don't understand. You must not leave us like this. We're women."

"Medlee, you're a very strong woman and plus, you're very independent."

"You don't get it, Tryess," she continued to say. "We're women. Every woman needs a man to lean on, a father, a husband, a brother, and even a son. You know how the life is like in this town. I fear nothing but evil souls. The bad people aren't dead." She paused for a moment. "Look, my husband is gone without leaving a trace. I don't know if he's alive or not. What if you and my son suddenly disappear in the ocean? Who's going to look after us? After Alessia and your baby that is coming soon… Yes, I am independent by nature but not to the society. You men don't think well enough like us. Perhaps, you men aren't treated like us. We're treated differently."

"You're right, Medlee," his wife agreed.

Arthur and his uncle stayed silent for a while. The silence struck in every corner of the house and empty echoes wandered around like ghosts.

Their life was tough. Men were meant to work in the town and not women. Single mothers, widows etc. would try to make a living by sewing dresses or working as a nurse or maid and such. There were a few opportunities for them to have an independent life. Small charities supported those women with money. And on the other hand, men would show up to those women when they'd see them without men to support them. They'd offer marriage or worse threaten them if they would say no.

Arthur's uncle finally attempted to speak.

"You're right, Sister," he continued to say, "anyways, thank you for the biscuits and the tea. I'll see you before leaving, tomorrow. Let's go, Alessia."

"You're not upset of what I said, are you? I hope you're not." Arthur's mother held her brother's hand.

"No, I'm not." He patted her hand. "Everything that you said is wise and there are many things I must learn from life. I thought I knew better about everything." Then he looked at her. "Medlee, if the trip would be successful, would you allow Arthur to go for a trip to the ocean next time?" he asked.

"Maybe. Everything happens on the right time. Brother, about the trip… Please make sure you come before the evening. Don't stay longer in the ocean or until the evening there."

"Right," he paused and said, "don't worry, we should arrive before the evening. Alright, we have to go."

Arthur's uncle and his wife said goodbye. Arthur and his mother waved to them as they watched them walking away.

They closed the door and right away Arthur's mother started to clean up and took the cups and plates to the kitchen. Arthur had nothing to do and the evening wasn't soon yet. *What should I do?* he wondered.

"Mother, do you need help in the kitchen?"

"No, Arthur."

"Okay, I'll water the flowers."

"I watered them this morning"

He sat down and was indeed bored. *Gosh, I have nothing to do at all.*

Someone knocked on the door just then. Arthur got up quickly to open it.

"Hey, buddy," Billy greeted Arthur.

"Hi, Billy!" He shook his hand.

"It's good to see you," Billy said.

"It's good to see you too," Arthur replied.

"Who's there?" Arthur's mother asked.

"It's Billy, Mother," Arthur said.

"Rude! Tell Billy to come in," his mother yelled.

"Yes, right, sorry. Please come in."

"No, I was thinking to go for a walk with you," Billy proposed.

Arthur's mother came close and said, "Billy, hello! Come in, son."

"Hello, Mrs. Byron. It's alright, maybe next time. I'd like to take a walk and hang out with Arthur if you don't mind?" Billy said.

"Yes, sure, as you like but next time you are going to come in and drink tea with us," Arthur's mother insisted.

"Sure thing. Thank you. See you, aunt," Billy said politely.

"See you. Take care, you two!" Arthur's mother said.

"We'll!" Arthur replied.

Arthur left the house and went to hang out with Billy.

"So, what are you up to?" Arthur asked Billy.

"Nothing. I saw you earlier in the great hall but we were sitting far and it was too crowded."

"Yes, true. Also, I didn't see your family."

"Yes, right. I came on my own."

"Did you see Peter or Robert there?"

"Yes, I saw Robert in the great hall and I saw Peter at the port."

"Robert was actually there…?" Arthur mumbled.

"Yes. What's wrong?" Billy was worried.

Could it be really him? Why did he do that to me? Arthur thought.

"Nothing. Forget about it. It's not important."

"Okay… So…"

"So?"

"Are you going tomorrow with the others to the ocean?"

"No, I have to stay and look after my mother. Also, I have to go to work in the afternoon."

"I see…"

"Peter and Robert are going, right?"

"Yes, and also me."

"You?! What…? What about Serina and your studies? You told me a while ago, you were preparing yourself to leave this week."

"I know, right, but I decided to postpone my studies for next year."

"May I ask why?"

"Well… You know, Lilly…" He fixed his glasses and continued to say, "The girl that I met in Serina."

"Yes, the girl you like?"

"Shh, don't say that out loud, I didn't tell anyone about her yet." He blushed.

Arthur chuckled. "Yes, sorry… What about her?"

"Well, she is finishing her studies this year and she'll continue her higher studies next year. So, I thought… To join next year and study with her and get to know her better meanwhile."

"That's actually a good idea and then once you two finish your studies…"

"Yes…?"

"Wedding!" Arthur teased him.

Billy laughed and said, "Sure thing, I'll be a married man then and have my own family; once I start to work as a teacher, yes."

"Yes, it'd be nice."

"What about you?" Billy asked.

"Me? About traveling?" Arthur was confused.

"No, any girl you like?"

"No, not really."

"You sure?"

"Yes, where would I meet a girl? I'm always working all week long and resting on the weekend."

"Maybe, you should go out more often on the weekend and you'll meet the one."

"The one, you said," Arthur shook his head and laughed.

"Why not?"

"Maybe one day, but for now all I want to do is help my mother and… I really want to wander around the world and…" Arthur sighed.

"And?"

"Find my father."

"Oh, don't worry, you will, hopefully."

"Billy, do you believe in sea monster and Oer—"

"Hey, hey… stop. We can't talk about this here."

"Why not? Why people don't dare to talk about this stuff?" Arthur said quietly.

"These tales are meant to be unspoken. People don't believe in them or they just want to forget. You know, my father once tried to speak about one of them with me at our house and he was looking over his shoulders, was worried if someone would hear him. It's worse to speak about it in public."

Arthur sighed. "I wish it was easier. I sometimes think that if we knew a little more about them, maybe I would find a clue to find my father."

"I see. You will, just wait and you'll be able to travel and hopefully meet your father again."

"I hope so too."

Billy placed his hand on Arthur's shoulder and smiled.

"You will, you will." Billy looked Arthur in the eye and said, "Just be patient."

Arthur nodded his head and smiled back at him. *I'm glad that I have a friend like him,* he thought.

6- Reunion

It had been two months since *Maxemus* sailed the ocean. The trip was successful. And ever since then, more ships started to sail the ocean and went fishing. In addition to that, people started trading across the seas as well. With Shellia specifically. It'd been a while, Arthur thought as the people would sail the ocean, they'd see Oernatus. However, nobody mentioned anything about Oernatus. Arthur asked his uncle and he told him that Oernatus might have disappeared due to a volcano and sunk or it was just abandoned. *I never understood what they meant by abandoned... How would a big country be abandoned or disappear?* At least, he mentioned the country name without being worried to be heard.

It got really boring for Arthur to go to work every day while he'd see his friends traveling every once in a while, and they asked him to join them several times but his mother wouldn't let him. Even Peter started to travel to trade their leathered products with his father and he even started going by his own too a few times when it was needed. The leather shop and tannery work expanded and the profit had risen. More people got hired to work there. One of those who were hired lately was Robert's older brother.

Robert's family and Billy's family were rich ones. Normally, they wouldn't have any interest in working normal jobs. They had their own business. However, Kevin, Robert's older brother, decided to work in the tannery because he was curious to learn something new, could be temporarily. He didn't like to spend all day in their carpet shops. Before getting this job, he worked in a butcher shop. Normally, people let him work because he'd ask for very low wage. So now, Kevin would work in the morning in the tannery, and in the afternoon, he'd check how the work's going in their carpet shop. They truly sold unique carpets and not anyone could buy them, only those who had their pockets full.

On the other hand, Billy's family had jewelry shops. They'd sell gold, silver, and sometimes they'd sell precious gemstones. He always wore a ring that had green gem on it. Billy and Robert were humble and never treated Arthur and Peter differently as both of them belonged to middle class.

Meanwhile, many things had changed around Arthur and he felt like the time had stopped on him. However, there's just one change that happened which was he had got a cousin now, after a long wait and a big hope. They named him Charlie. Arthur's uncle and his wife weren't able to have children and it finally came true now. Every evening, Arthur and his mother would go and see him growing up little by little. Arthur liked to give him his finger and he'd hold his finger with his whole hand. *I love his tiny hands and feet. I can't believe that I was once this tiny before,* Arthur would think to himself.

Other than that, nothing had changed for him. He felt like he was waiting in line but he would never reach what he wanted because there was no line to stand in. He didn't know when he'd ever be able to travel... *I can't just stay here, I want to travel, I have many questions in my head that need answers...*

"Argh!" Arthur accidentally cut his finger with the scissors.

"Are you okay?" Mr. Lomar asked.

"Yes... It's my fault. I wasn't paying attention."

"Your finger's bleeding, here, take this napkin," Mr. Lomar handed him the napkin. "Cover it well."

"Thank you."

"You have been overthinking recently. I noticed that you space out more often. Arthur, is everything okay with you?"

"Yes. I just shouldn't be overthinking when I am working."

"I understand." Mr. Lomar paused and thought to himself a little but then finally spoke, "Arthur, I was thinking to send Peter again with Kevin to Shellia to trade our products there, the leathered shoes that you were making. People of Shellia admired them. I was wondering, would you like to join them? It'd be nice to learn how to trade and to discover a new country," Mr. Lomar suggested.

"Me? Yes, but... I can't."

"Is it because you have to work at Jones' stables or your mother wouldn't allow you to?"

"Well, I need to stay and look after my mother."

"Talk to her and let me know if she accepts or not. I think you need to travel once in a while."

"I bet."

"Arthur, you can go home. You need to rest. I can continue this."

"No, I will finish it up. I am almost done."

"No, listen to elders. Go, son, and let me know if you can go to Shellia this Friday."

Arthur nodded. "Thank you, sir."

He put the scissors aside and left.

As Arthur was on his way back home, he was thinking of what to say to his mother but his mind was blank and out of ideas.

He knocked on the door, his mother opened it.

"Are you okay? You're early," his mother was worried.

"Yes, I finished working early."

"Wait, what happened to your hand?" his mother looked at his finger covered with a napkin.

"Nothing, it's just my finger…" he got inside the house.

"What happened?" his mother closed the door.

"I wasn't concentrating and I accidentally cut my finger with the scissors. It's just a small wound."

"Let me clean it for you."

"It's okay, I can do it by myself, Mother. I'll take a bath and then I'll clean it."

"Is everything alright with you?"

"Yes, I'm just tired I guess," he excused himself to go to take a bath.

Once he was done bathing and dressing up, he cleaned the wound and wrapped it up with a bandage.

The food was already on the table. It was grilled fish with vegetable stew and rice. As people started to go fishing more often lately; the price of the fish became fair and possible for anyone to buy. Arthur too was able to buy fish every once in a while.

Funny fact, my father is a fisherman and I buy fish now… I should be fishing instead of just buying fish. He was being hard on himself.

"Son, come on, let's eat," his mother said.

Arthur nodded his head and he pulled the chair and sat down.

They were eating and neither of them was talking. They never minded being quiet but this silence was awkwardly uncomfortable for both of them.

"I'll take some food for Alessia and Tryess," his mother attempted to break the silence.

"Mhm."

"Are you coming to see Charlie after you're done from work?"

"No, I'll stay home this evening."

"Son, are you really alright?"

"Yes… I'm just tired."

"Tired?"

"I don't know, it's either tired or I'm bored… Simply both."

"Mhm."

"Mhm."

"Arthur, is Peter going to travel soon? You know for trading leather goods of his father's shop?" his mother asked.

"Yes, Peter and Kevin are going this Friday."

"Do you want to go with them?"

"Well, I don't know. I no longer know what I want." Arthur put his fork down on the plate. "Well, in fact…" he sighed. "Mr. Lomar asked me to go with them to Shellia in order to learn about trading and get to know the place there."

"Sure, you can go."

"Then I was thinking that maybe I... What? Did you just say I can go?"

"Yes, you can go with them," his mother smiled.

"Really? Like really, Mother?" Arthur said and he was fully surprised.

"Yes, or do you want me to change my mind?" his mother joked.

"No, don't, please don't. I really want to go."

"Good. It's good to see you all excited again, you should go soon and let Mr. Lomar know about it and make sure to talk with Mr. Jones first to take Friday off."

"Yes, I will." Arthur got up.

"Son! Where are you going? Sit down, continue eating."

"Oh, right. I think I got too excited." He rubbed his hair.

His mother laughed at him and he laughed too.

Arthur sat down and ate. His appetite returned and he started to eat with joy. And his heart – oh his heart was filled with happiness and he felt as if he woke up into life again. He couldn't wait, his heart was beating fast for a new adventure. It felt like a dream was about to come true for him.

After they finished eating, Arthur accompanied his mother to his uncle's house and carried the food. As they arrived there, they greeted his uncle's wife and Arthur kissed Charlie on his forehead as he was still sleeping. His uncle wasn't there because he was still at work. He'd come home soon to have his lunch break. Arthur excused himself and took his leave to work at Jones' stables.

The rest of the day had passed really quickly for Arthur. Perhaps it was because he was too thrilled about going for another trip. He wasn't even feeling tired after work. He asked Mr. Jones to have the Friday off and he accepted. On his way back, he stopped to tell Peter about it, so he could tell his father too.

As he walked back home, he was thinking, *I will finally see the ocean for the first time. People told me you wouldn't notice any difference, it's all water but one is deeper than the other. I will try to notice something different about it and maybe find a trail about the truth of it.*

Friday – Dawn Time

It was finally Friday. Arthur wore his clothes and got ready quickly. He left his room and he didn't see his mother in the living room or in the kitchen.

"Mother? Are you awake?" Arthur called her.

"Yes, I woke up. I'm in my room," she answered.

He knocked on her room's door. "Can I come in?"

"Yes, please."

He looked around and he didn't see her. Then his mother's head appeared from under the bed.

"Please come help me."

"Oh… yes… what should I do?" Arthur was confused.

"There's a chest under the bed, can you try to pull it out for me… It's heavier than I thought."

"Alright."

He bowed on his knees and pulled this wooden chest. *Oh God, it's too heavy. I thought it'd be less heavy than this.* He used all his strength and finally pulled it out.

"This is… This is too heavy," said Arthur, trying to catch his breath.

"I'm sorry, son," his mother said and she caressed his shoulder.

"It… It's okay."

His mother opened the chest. He looked curiously inside. There were only table clothes and blankets. His mother took out some of the clothes and blankets until he saw a necklace, a red shiny stone and a silver chain. It didn't look like it belonged to his mother. It didn't look florally designed nor anything girly. *Maybe my father wore it before?*

She took it out and handed Arthur the necklace.

"For me?" he hesitated.

"Yes, take it and wear it."

"I don't get it… Why do I have to wear it, mother? Is it a present?"

"Don't ask a lot and just wear it." She took his hand and put the necklace in his hand.

It seemed like he had no choice but obey the command. He wore it. It looked actually good on him.

"Did this necklace belong to my father?"

"No," his mother said. She closed the chest and sat down on it.

"It belonged to my great grandfather. I actually saw my grandfather wearing it before. After he passed away, my father gave it to me," she said.

Wow, this is a real history around my neck! Arthur thought.

"It doesn't look old at all," Arthur said and kept touching it.

"Be careful when you touch it. Touch it gently and hide it under your shirt. Don't let others see it and if they see it and ask you to let them try it on, don't let them."

"Mother, what's this all about? I can't be quiet and not ask any questions. This is too suspicious and mysterious. I want to know about it."

His mother nodded her head. "I must tell you. My family believes that this necklace can keep whoever wears it safe. It's not the necklace itself but the red stone. This stone is a rare one. It was found in Sharona desert, it's in far west. And under me in this chest, there's a big stone. There are only two of them…"

Someone knocked on the front door.

"That must be Peter. He can wait, please tell me more."

"No, let's go to the port. We shouldn't be late or else you'd miss the ship."

"But, Mother, please promise me you'd tell me all about it when I'm back."

"I will. Remind me of it if I forget to tell you."

"Yes…"

Peter knocked on the door again.

"Do you need me to push it back under the bed?"

"No, leave it this way. Go, open the door," his mother said and covered the chest with a table cloth.

He went and opened the door.

"Good morning, Arthur, don't be late. I'll meet you at the port," Peter said in rush.

Arthur looked behind Peter and saw the horse carriage. Mr. Lomar and Kevin were riding in it. They waved at Arthur and said, "Good morning!"

"Good morning," Arthur replied.

"I will get on the carriage. You need to help us to lift the shipment to the ship, okay?" Peter said.

"Okay."

"Hurry up."

Arthur nodded his head.

He turned back and his mother was standing right behind him. She handed him his bag.

"I will accompany you."

Arthur nodded and they left home together.

The sky was still grey, the sun hadn't woken up yet. They could see the shy blue had started to move over the greyness of the sky as they arrived by the port. Arthur saw that everything was well prepared and all he had to do was lift the goods to the ship. Peter, Kevin, and Arthur carried the shipment all together because it was quite heavy. They placed them in the right place and once they were done, he excused himself to say goodbye to his mother.

His mother was standing with his uncle.

"Son, look after yourself," his mother said.

"I will," he hugged her and kissed her on the cheeks.

"My nephew, oh my nephew, here's your dream come true. Have fun!" He tackled him with a strong hug.

"Ah… I will. Thank you… I can't breathe, Uncle!"

His uncle laughed and finally let go.

"I must leave now… I'll see you tonight."

"May God keep you safe."

"May God keep you safe as well, goodbye."

He walked toward the ship and out of the blue, someone called Arthur and dragged him backward from his arm.

"What? ROBERT!" Arthur looked behind him. He also saw Billy. "BILLY, you're here too!" Arthur was surprised and happy.

"Man, did you see his reaction?" Robert said.

"Are you guys coming with us?"

"Sure, man. We're coming with you," Robert said.

"Really?"

"Yes, really, Arthur. You're really surprised! We're glad we got you this time!" Billy said.

They got on the ship together. Peter got up and greeted them. He didn't look surprised about seeing them.

"You knew that they're coming with us, right?" Arthur asked Peter.

"Yes, Billy and Robert wanted to surprise you."

"It was Robert's idea actually. I wanted to tell you about it but he told us to keep it a secret and surprise you," Billy spoke.

"What do you think about this surprise, Arthur?" Robert asked and smiled at Arthur.

"It's the best! I'm very happy! Thank you, guys!"

"Sure thing, look at his smile. He's grinning from ear to ear," Peter said.

They all laughed at him and he couldn't help but laugh foolishly with them. *I'm really happy to see all of us together. I finally got to see Robert after a long time. He looks better than before. I'm glad for him.*

The ship just started to sail away and Arthur watched his mother and uncle still standing there and waving at him and his friends. Arthur and his friends waved back to them.

It's always nice to travel and it's nicer to travel with friends, Arthur mused.

However, there was a little thing that bothered Arthur; that he was traveling by a regular ship. He wished to travel by *Maxemus*. He heard that it was fast and furious like a shark. Yet, people of Lillianta agreed to sail by *Maxemus* just on special events and important occasions. In order to keep it in a good shape, and just in case if any war would start. It seemed to be peaceful and nobody thought of any war would begin.

But Arthur's uncle told him, "It's always better to stay aware and careful because now our relations have expanded with other countries."

The sun was about to rise. Arthur leaned on the handrail and gazed at the sea. Slowly, the colors of the sunrise were being painted over the sea. Arthur started to wander into his thoughts about the ocean and what people had said about it. *The ocean's too secretive, far away and out of our reach. It's never calm and it's never quiet. They say "There's a creature in the ocean that can take away people's lives" and some say "that creature is a monster". There are many tales they have hidden about the ocean. Just few parts of it are little known, which leaves me confused and blurred. Is the ocean harmful? Or is there really an ocean monster? I can't tell until I go there. I hope I'd find a clue.*

Dolphins. Dolphins distracted Arthur's thoughts and brought him back to where he stood. He was amazed by them and how beautifully they swam beside the ship. *Perhaps, they are greeting us or wishing us a safe trip.*

Someone hit Arthur's shoulder. "Oow…"

"Come on, it didn't hurt," Robert said.

"I know but you kinda scared me that wasn't expected."

"Yes, I had to interrupt what you were doing."

"What was I doing?"

"Your usual thing; staring, gazing, and observing nature and everything. Thinking about life."

Arthur shrugged. "I think this thing lives in me."

"You never change."

"You never change either."

"No, I've changed. Look at those muscles, and you gained none." Robert showed him his big bicep muscles and smirked.

"Oh well," Arthur sighed.

"I'm just joking with you, man," he continued to say, "here, take this. You probably didn't eat. I made one for you." He handed Arthur a loaf of bread filled with tuna and salad and a sort of sauce. It looked delicious.

"For me? Since when do you make food?"

"Since I started traveling. Taste it and tell me if you like it."

"Okay."

Arthur was just about to take a bite. The ship suddenly shook and the sandwich fell off from his hands and it dropped in the sea.

"Damn. This must be the ocean curse," Robert said.

"Ocean curse? Did we even reach the ocean?"

"Yes, or almost there. I don't know, not much of time has passed but look how big the waves are!"

"Right... I'm sorry that your sandwich fell from my hands."

"It's okay. It's just a sandwich."

Robert looked a little disappointed and was quiet for a few seconds.

"Let's go in, maybe the guys have some food too but hey, wait. I gotta tell you something."

"What's it?" Arthur was curious.

"Don't you dare to tell anyone, okay? This is a secret. Well, the guys kinda knew or had guesses but I confirmed none."

"Jeez, just tell me already. What is it?"

"I met a fine lady, Arthur."

"Really?"

"Yup, in Shellia. I think she got my heart."

"Wow, you're in love!?"

"I wouldn't deny. Men do fall in love and there's no shame in it."

"True."

"I'll try to be a better person, just for her. Listen, keep your eyes open, you might find a girl that will steal your heart too."

"I don't know. I am just here to learn trading and…"

"Hey, stop right there. You would give the shipment once you got there but then there would be plenty of time to discover the place and see the beauty of the place and… beautiful girls, you know what I mean?"

"Jeez, Robert!" Arthur chuckled. "I wasn't planning for the last part you mentioned, I just…"

Robert interrupted Arthur. "Nah, love isn't a planned thing. It just happens. Alright?"

"I agree."

"Yeah? Alright, let's join the guys and your mouth," Robert made a gesture over his mouth, "zip it."

"Got it." Arthur covered his mouth for a second.

"I guessed it zipped well," Robert said then laughed and Arthur laughed too.

"Shall we go in?"

"Yeah, let's go."

7- Shellia

Arthur woke up to a sound of shouting. He thought that some people were fighting. He opened his eyes, terrified. He tried to look around him but it was only Kevin; shouting, trying to wake him and Peter up.

"Why are you shouting like this?" Peter asked as he started to blink his eyes open.

"I called your names for long, and you'd not wake up. I had to do it this way," Kevin told them.

"But… still… This is not a good way," Arthur said.

"Don't be like spoiled kids now, get up. Everyone is leaving the ship and Mr. Lentoz is already waiting us at the port. We have to give the shipment to him."

"Where's Robert? Where's Billy?" Arthur asked then he just saw Billy walked down the stairs.

"Do you need any help, guys?" Billy offered help.

"Oh, yes please! You can carry one or two of those packages only," Kevin said.

"Sure," Billy said and he fixed his glasses on his nose well, so they'd not fall off.

Arthur finally got up on his feet and he gave his hand to Peter to help him getting up too. He started carrying the shipment together with Kevin and Peter. It was not a great way of waking up at all and carrying heavy goods too soon but a job had to be done.

They carried them all the way to Mr. Lentoz's carriage and put them there.

"At 3 o'clock, you guys should be here," the captain of the ship told Arthur and his friends.

"Yes, we'll be on time," Kevin said.

Arthur finally got to meet Mr. Lentoz for the first time. Kevin and Peter used to talk about Mr. Lentoz to Arthur and made fun of his big moustache, he remembered the jokes they told about him; "You must see his big moustache, I bet people will pay him to get his hair to use them as strings for their guitars," and seeing him with this huge moustache, Arthur couldn't help but laugh while greeting him. He felt ashamed and his cheeks were on fire but he just couldn't stop himself. Mr. Lentoz was a kind person and he was cheerful too. He laughed along without knowing what was the reason for it.

"You must be a joyful guy," Mr. Lentoz said with an accent and laughed with Arthur.

"I guess," Arthur chuckled. "Sorry, I'm just too excited to meet you." Arthur finally managed to stop laughing somewhat.

"Me too," Mr. Lentoz said and smiled at him.

Peter covered his face with his arm to prevent himself from laughing as he knew why Arthur was laughing!

"You guys finally got off the ship," Robert said.

"Where have you been? You didn't want to give us a hand, did you?" Kevin said.

"Oh brother, why wouldn't I help? I just needed to go to the toilet," Robert claimed.

"We'll have to talk later. Let's go now. Shall we go Mr. Lentoz?" Kevin asked.

"Yes," Mr. Lentoz replied. He got up on his carriage and was ready to ride it. "Heyo!" he said to his donkeys to begin to move.

Arthur and his friends followed Mr. Lentoz by foot. The donkeys weren't fast and it was almost easy to not lose track of the carriage. As they entered the city through the great gates, women and kids threw roses before them. Arthur felt shy, this was a really warm welcome for him. He didn't expect this. Arthur tried to avoid stepping on the roses as much as possible.

"What are you doing?" Billy asked Arthur.

"I don't want to step on the roses."

Billy laughed. "This is impossible, there are everywhere on the ground. I tried to avoid them the first time I came here but I ended up bumping into a man and he got too angry at me. Just walk and pretend there are no roses there."

"I will try to think this way while walking. Even though it's difficult. Do they always welcome people this way?"

"I heard, it's only on Friday, Saturday, and Sunday they'd do such welcoming like this around this time. So, we're lucky to come on this time."

"Yes, I'm glad we made it on time. By the way, how long you're going to stay in Shellia?"

"I am not staying. I will go back with you. Robert will stay until Monday."

"He's staying until Monday? He's lucky," Peter joined the conversation.

"I bet he wants to stay longer to see his lover," Kevin said.

"What? He likes someone?" Peter asked.

"Who's she?" Billy asked.

"I am not sure but… Shh, he's around. I can't say more," Kevin said.

Robert came close to them. "Hey, were you talking about me? You suddenly went quiet!"

"Yes, I was telling them how you have become not useful."

"Come on, just because this time I didn't help picking up things with you. And listen, it is not even my job. I'm here to have fun and accompany my friends."

"Hey, I'm older than you, watch out how you speak."

"Guys, please don't fight. Robert is right, we're here to have fun too, not only work," Arthur said, "and look, Mr. Lentoz's quite ahead of us. If we stop like this, we would be too late."

"Right," Kevin said.

They started to walk in a faster pace but that didn't stop Arthur from looking around. He fell in love with the structures of the buildings. They looked quite huge and historical. He brushed his tip fingers on the dusty walls as they walked by them, it gave him a sort of emotion like he was making contact with the history.

The walls were too hard, they were built of bricks. He looked up and the buildings were too tall. *How could they build high buildings like this?*

Suddenly, Mr. Lentoz stopped his carriage and said loudly "Guards are passing. Guards are passing."

"What did he say? Why have you all stopped here?" Arthur didn't hear what Mr. Lentoz said as he was distracted by the beauty of the buildings.

He walked up closely and suddenly a leopard was about to attack him. He froze in his spot and Peter pulled him back and they both fell on the ground. Arthur was still and couldn't move. It felt like he just had a heart attack. Two guards pulled the chains tightly, so the leopard would back off. This all happened quickly in seconds and the time froze with Arthur. He got scared to the point that he didn't notice that the leopard was chained when it was about to jump toward him. *I thought it was really going to attack me.*

Finally, all the guards passed by and there were men who dressed differently from the guards. They were wearing big heavy armors.

"What... what—what was that?" Arthur barely put words together to form a question.

"That was a tiger!" Billy said as he reached to them and gave them his hands to help them get up.

Kevin came and asked them if they're okay. Both of them nodded their heads.

"A tiger?" *I guess I couldn't tell the difference between the tiger and leopard from being scared.* "Why was the tiger with the guards? I don't get it," Arthur spoke his thoughts loudly.

"It's for a fight. Strong fighters go enter in the field and fight against wild animals," Peter said.

"Fighters?" Arthur wondered.

"Gladiators. Have you heard or read about Gladiators?" Billy asked.

"Yes... I thought that was like ages ago and people are no longer having this..." Arthur replied.

"Well, it's still going on here. The gladiators are the ones that were wearing big heavy armors," Peter explained.

Arthur remembered the necklace! He touched his neck and his chest. *It's still there.* He let a sigh of relief.

"I see… Hey, Peter… Thank you, buddy. You saved my life! That tiger was really close to get me."

"Oh, don't thank me. We're brothers." He put his arm on Arthur's shoulders and walked together.

"Yes, we're brothers." Arthur smiled and was a little emotional.

He was very thankful to have his friends around him and how they were family to him.

Shortly after, they arrived at Mr. Lentoz's store and they helped him again to place the goods there. Billy and Kevin waited outside while Arthur and Peter sat in Mr. Lentoz's office; he counted the money in front of them and gave the money to Peter and then Peter put the money inside his bag. Now, the job was officially done.

Now it was time to finally enjoy the trip. They continued discovering the place. Arthur's friends had already discovered it before him but surely there were still places that they didn't discover about Shellia yet and they could still explore more.

They entered the shops area, it felt cozy. Arthur saw lovely silver earrings that caught his attention quickly. He asked the guys to stop and wait for him for a little bit while he'd check those earrings.

"Those ones are special, my friend. It was designed carefully and made with PURE silver," the salesman said with an accent. Arthur noticed that Shellian people sort of had an accent when they spoke Lilliantian language and he admired it.

Arthur looked at them and they looked really beautiful. At same time, he felt this guy was saying lots of overwhelming words to get him to buy them. He sighed and thought deeply.

"Trust me, my friend. You will look in all other shops and you won't find earrings like those, trust me," salesman said.

Billy entered the shop and looked at the earrings.

"Those look nice, are you buying them for your mother?" Billy asked.

"Yes."

"You know, my family and I have a jewelry shop, you can always come and buy from us. I can make discount for you," Billy whispered to him.

Arthur chuckled. "I know, right… But those caught my attention so much," he spoke in a quiet voice.

"Mind if I touch them?" Billy asked the salesman.

"Go ahead."

Billy took the earrings in his hand and he looked closely at them. Then finally Billy put the earrings on the counter.

"Arthur, I think we should go. Peter is hungry, we need to go," Billy said and rose one of his eyebrows as a gesture to leave from here.

"But…" Arthur didn't get it.

"Gentleman, I can drop the price for you. What about 20 dons?" salesman said.

"Arthur, this isn't pure silver. It was mixed with other metals, it should be cheaper than this. And with time, it would break," Billy said in very low tone.

"I'm sorry sir. We have to go; it is an urgent thing," Billy told the salesman.

"Yes, we have to go. Sorry," Arthur said.

"Come on, gentlemen. What about 18 dons?" the salesman said.

"Just walk, don't look back. He eventually would stop talking to us."

They walked ahead without looking back and Arthur dragged Peter from his arm. "Let's go."

"Okay," Peter said and walked with them in a quick pace without knowing why they were in a rush and Kevin followed them.

"Gentlemen, 15 dons! For only 15 dons!" salesman yelled outside his shop.

They had gone too far already.

"10 dons! 10 dons!" salesman yelled and hit the door with anger.

Everyone was hungry and they stopped at a restaurant in the area. They knew this restaurant, the guys kept telling Arthur about it earlier. They told him that they had great seafood and best lemonade. Robert showed up out of nowhere and he was talking to the waitress aside. He was standing too close to her. The girl looked upset for some reason and when he saw his friends, he took a step back from her then joined them.

"Lousina, please I'd like to order the usual," Robert said and sat down with them.

She nodded her head.

"What about you guys?" she asked.

"We'd like to have a full seafood meal but we'd like the fish to be fried. And for the drinks, we'd like lemonade, right?" Billy said and looked at them.

Peter and Kevin nodded their heads in agreement.

"What about you, new guy?" Lousina asked and she looked at Arthur straight in the eye.

He looked at her and he was confused of the way she was looking at him. He looked at the menu right away and wasn't sure what to order. "Yes, just like what my friends ordered and lemonade too please."

"Alright," she wrote down the orders on a tiny note and left.

"What's the usual, Robert?" Kevin was curious.

"Grilled fish with vegetable stew with a refreshing…" Robert said and saw a paper on the ground.

"Refreshing what?" Kevin asked.

Robert picked up the paper and stood up with excitement.

"Look guys, there's a fight today. Guys, let's go watch the fight. Tiger vs Gladiators. It is the main event of the day," Robert said in a loud tone.

"That's cool. Let's go after lunch, what do you say guys?" Peter said.

"No, we'd be late," Kevin said and looked at his pocket watch.

"No, they will not be late! Arthur, Billy, come on?" Robert asked.

"I… I don't know. I don't think I want to see a fight," Arthur replied.

"Oh, don't be a chicken," Robert mocked him.

"Well, I'd not like to go either. I want to show Arthur the red trees," Billy responded.

"Man, who cares about trees now? Well, here's another chicken," Robert said and he made chicken noise.

"You're the real chicken now with all those noises," Kevin said and laughed.

"Don't make fun of..." Robert stopped talking once Lousina came with the drinks.

"Gentlemen, here are your drinks," Lousina said and placed each glass in front of them.

Until it was Arthur's turn, she placed the glass and said, "Here's your lemonade, shy guy." And then she smiled at him and left.

Arthur was being awkward and he rubbed the back of his head. His friends looked at him and burst into laughter.

"What? Why are you guys laughing?" Arthur was questioning.

"You're blushing, man. Look at him," Peter said and laughed.

"Do you like her?" Billy asked.

"No!" Arthur shook his head.

"I bet he liked her right away," Kevin said.

"N-No, no, guys, stop! I don't even know her. It was just awkward... I was confused why she was treating me this way, that's all!" Arthur explained.

They continued laughing. "We know. We're just teasing you," and eventually everyone just started to chill... Except for Robert, he looked a little mad or nervous. He kept tapping his foot and it made the table shake a little bit too.

Lousina and a guy came to place the food. Arthur looked at his plate; there was a fried fish with some fried potatoes, some shrimps with tomato sauce on the side and mussels with lemon. He grabbed one of the mussels and it started to jiggle and it looked very sticky. It was not even cooked. It smelled like the sea on a hot sunny day! He looked at Billy as he grabbed one and squeezed a lemon over it then swallowed it and put the shell aside.

Brr, it gives me a chilly feeling and shudder from watching this. Argh, I think I will keep that for later, I'll start from the fish!

Arthur enjoyed the meal except for the mussels, he didn't even touch them again. The lemonade was refreshing and fancy. Everyone paid for their meal and they left. Arthur noticed that Robert was in a bad mood and he told the guys that maybe they should just watch the fight with Robert. And indeed, his mood got way better. He and Peter shouted at the top of their lungs with the crowd while Kevin sat next to them and watched it quietly. Billy and Arthur sat in the back in order to avoid looking at most of what was happening in the field. They didn't like violence and it was too disturbing to watch for them.

I don't know how people can enjoy this and I don't believe that people are still allowing fights like this. It's harmful for the gladiators and the wild animals as they'd end up being injured or sadly killed. It is sad to see livings used for an entertainment.

After two fights were done, they really had to leave as the time passed quickly. They left running.

"Why we have to run each time? Why we have to be late?" Peter said.

They arrived a little late and they were breathless. Peter was checking his bag to make sure if the money was there after the crazy run. They looked and saw that people were just sitting on the ground and waiting. They asked them and they told them that the crew and the captain were trying to repair the ship and this would take some time. Arthur and his friends went to drink water which was set for free for the sailors and visitors at the port.

Then they sat down and waited. Billy pulled a book out of his bag.

It's a good idea to read while waiting but I didn't bring any books with me, thought Arthur. He asked Billy if he had another book with him. Luckily, he brought another book with him and he gave it to Arthur to read.

While Arthur was reading, he was worried if the ship wouldn't be repaired but at the same time, he wanted to stay the night. He wanted to see the waterfalls that his friends told him about before and also the red trees. They were unique type of trees that only grew in Shellia. There were many things to see in Shellia and unfortunately, Arthur and his friends didn't have the time on their side.

8- The Necklace

Arthur read the inked words, page after page. He yawned and put down the book. He saw that people had started to get on the ship. *Why nobody told us?* He looked at Billy and he was lying down on the ground and the book was covering his face. Peter was sleeping while cuddling his bag. He had to protect it and the money in it even when he was asleep. Kevin wasn't around and neither was Robert. Robert was going to stay in Shellia for a few days but Kevin was supposed to be around to go back home with them.

"Billy, wake up!" Arthur said.

"I'm awake. I'm just resting my eyes. I read too much," Billy said.

"Well, open your eyes and get up. People are getting on the ship already."

"Okay…" Billy slowly got up.

"Wake up, Peter… Peter!"

"I hear-r you!" Peter answered. "I slept a lot today."

"Here," Arthur handed Billy the book. "Thank you."

"You can keep it for a while, if you want to," Billy replied.

"That's alright. I am afraid to keep it and don't have the time to read. It's better that it stays with you."

"Okay but know that you can borrow it anytime," Billy said and took the book.

"Let's go, guys. Wait, where's Kevin?" Peter said.

"I don't know. I was wondering the same thing. Maybe he got on the ship before us," Arthur said.

"Let's look for him there," Billy suggested.

They looked inside the ship. They asked the people in it and they said they hadn't seen Kevin and neither his brother. They went to the captain and asked him to wait for little longer while they go and search for them. The captain only agreed to wait half an hour because the sun was setting and it'd get dark.

As they were leaving the ship, they saw Kevin and Robert walking toward them. Robert's shirt had a little blood on it. It looked like he was in a fight. Kevin seemed to be in a bad mood.

"Are you okay guys?" Billy asked.

"Yes."

"Yeah."

"Where have you been?" Peter asked.

"Just around. I had to look after my little brother."

"You didn't have to."

"You're coming with us?" Arthur asked Robert.

"Yes, and stop questioning us. Let us get in," Robert said.

"Yeah… right," Billy said.

They all got on the ship and Arthur seriously needed to sleep. Reading made him sleepy even though the book wasn't bad. He headed downstairs to find a place to rest and sleep but Robert grabbed him from his arm.

"Can we talk for a second?" Robert asked Arthur.

"Sure…"

The guys and other people got inside. The captain and his assistant were on the deck. Robert walked slowly toward the handrail and leaned on it. He was looking at the waves and how slowly the waves' color turned into grey as it was almost evening.

"Are you okay?" Arthur asked.

"Yes, just tired."

"I see."

"And I'm not going to lie; I drank a little. I wish I could stop this habit when I'm in a rough mood," Robert said.

"There's blood on your shirt. Did you get into a fight while you got drunk?"

"No, but my brother saw me drinking. We both were mad and we fought a little. He didn't want me to drink."

"Sorry to hear that." Arthur paused then continued to say, "Robert, you could talk to me and open up about what bothers you instead of drinking. If not me, anyone who you feel comfortable to talk to. Or even… you know… You could talk with her about it," Arthur said in a quiet voice, "the girl you like."

Robert got angry and his relaxing hand became stressed into a fist. He bit his hand and he opened it up.

"Forget it," Robert said. "I'll be alright. I think you're tired. Go, sleep. I will come to rest later." He was still not looking at Arthur. He was only looking at the ocean.

Arthur noticed Robert's anger and that he didn't look alright. He was worried and he didn't know what to say to him.

"Why you're still standing here? Go," Robert said.

"I thought you wanted to talk to me about something else."

"I said all what I had to say…"

"Alright… well, I will be inside."

"Yup. I will be here breathing some fresh air for little while."

"Okay… See you then."

Arthur walked away, looking on the ground, thinking if Robert would be alright on his own. *Maybe, I should stay up for little bit until he comes in to rest.*

"Hey, Arthur?"

"Yes, Robert?" Arthur turned to look at him.

"Forgive me for everything, man."

"You did nothing wrong to me though."

"Just say that you have forgiven me," Robert finally looked at Arthur in the eye.

"I forgive you. You know, you're like my brother."

Robert nodded his head and he looked up, trying to hold back the tears. "Thank you," he mumbled.

Arthur nodded his head. "Okay, don't be late. So you find a good spot to sleep on."

"Yeah!"

Arthur went inside. He saw Billy was fast asleep, Kevin as well. Peter was still up but he looked too tired and sleepy. Arthur lay down and tried to keep his eyes open. He waited for Robert to come inside. He waited, he was fighting his sleepiness and he waited, until he couldn't keep his eyes open…

All of sudden, Arthur heard Robert's screaming for help. He got up and ran up the stairs. The ship was empty. Arthur shouted, "Where are you, Robert?!"

He looked around and his heart was beating fast.

"Down… in the ocean. Help!"

Arthur saw Robert was drowning, struggling to swim. *He must have lost balance and fell off. I shouldn't have left him alone.* Arthur found a rope on the floor and threw it while still holding it in order to pull Robert but the waves pushed him back away. Arthur yelled for help but no one was hearing him. He found another rope, he tied it around his waist and around the metal handrail and he jumped into the water. He swam toward Robert and he came close to him.

"Robert, take my hand," Arthur shouted.

"I CAN'T!" Robert shouted back.

"TAKE MY HAND!"

"I CAN'T... I CANNOT, ARTHUR!"

Something pulled Robert down in the ocean and he disappeared.

Arthur gasped and woke up. "Thank God, it was just a dream," he mumbled.

Arthur was sweating. He took a napkin out of his pocket and with a shaking hand, he wiped his forehead and face. He looked around him, everyone was still sleeping. He looked carefully; he didn't see Robert among all the people. Arthur got up quickly and went on deck.

Arthur overheard the captain and his assistants talking.

"Captain, are you sure we're heading in the right direction? It's all dark. I see nothing... our compass is lost somewhere..." the assistant said.

"Yes, I have sailed during nights before. But tonight's darker than expected... There's something weird about it," the captain said.

"Captain! Captain! I think we're sailing further west. Look there, the whirlpools and the waves are too strong.

That's why it's too dark… These are the signs… We're near to Oernatus," the assistant shouted.

"Oh my God. We should head the opposite side. How did that happen? Did you turn the wheel around when I was gone for little while?" the captain said and tried to turn the ship's wheel.

"I DID NOT! I was away too."

"It isn't spinning, HELP ME!" the captain shouted.

The assistant was trying to help the captain to steer the wheel. Arthur was curious and went near the handrail. He saw huge waves; he never seen something like this and several of the whirlpools were almost near the ship. Slowly, all these whirlpools got together, making one massive whirlpool. It looked like a massive black hole in the ocean! Arthur's feet froze; *I don't know if I can run or hide. It looks like this whirlpool will swallow us!*

Suddenly, the ship started to move to the left and right continuously. Arthur tried so hard to hang on the handrail; in fact, he was literally embracing it with all his strength. Closing his eyes and praying so hard. It continued to move to the left and right.

Until it calmed down for a few moments… *I think it's all good now.* Arthur let go of the handrail and a strong wave hit the ship and he fell off but he managed to hang on the ledge, trying so hard to climb back up. He shouted for help.

"Robert… Robert… Help! Help me, Billy, Peter, Peter… Anyone, please help me, I am falling." He felt his hand was going to slip and cannot hang on for more "Billy, Billy. Captain… Captain, help!" he shouted at the top of his lungs. Then he looked down and his mouth was wide open… frightened of what he was seeing… The whirlpool was getting quite closer and closer toward the ship. Arthur looked up and was just about to shout for help once more but he saw a leathered boot stepping on his fingers with lots of hatred and Arthur fell off...

Arthur tried to swim and fight this whirlpool for life. It was not that easy at all. He was sucked in, being spun around endlessly, being pulled from all sides. He nearly gave up but his arms and legs weren't giving up, they kept moving. He closed his eyes; *My necklace*, he remembered. He placed his hand on his neck, it was still there. It was his last hope and he kept his hand over it, so it wouldn't tear off or get lost in the water. His throat burned, his lungs were in pain. He kept his eyes closed. He didn't want to see his end. *If it's happening, I don't want to see it.*

Arthur suddenly felt the pain slowly calming. He could breathe. He dared to open his eyes one more time. He found himself in the deepest spot of the ocean. His feet touched the sand. The whirlpool almost stopped. *How am I still alive and not out of breath? How am I breathing under water? I don't understand; am I alive or dead? What's happening to me?* He felt something was moving and touching the back of his legs, he looked back and he saw a giant long tail was moving around him. Turning around, he still didn't know what it was. It created another whirlpool again; *I can't see,* he thought.

Unexpectedly, the whirlpool stopped again and he slowly opened his eyes... he couldn't believe what he was seeing. A huge monster's moving too quickly toward him.

Arthur tried to swim up, but it was too late; it reached him in the blink of an eye and Artur failed to move again.

He was face to face with the ocean monster. It was the most frightening thing he had ever seen in his life. *Please*

God, wake me up from this nightmare! His heart was jumping and his head hurt.

The ocean monster had two huge eyes, horns that shaped like a crown, a huge mouth and sharpened teeth. It was too massive and long looking, like the longest snake, and its fins looked like dragon's wings.

The ocean monster looked at him closely. *Is it going to swallow me, eat me, or let go off me? I can't fight it and I can't escape it and I don't know how possibly I can even magically breathe under water. Seriously, what's happening…? Please God, save me.* Arthur just couldn't dare to make a move and the ocean monster still glared at him.

"Why are you here? Are you planning to do harm to me?" ocean monster spoke with a deep and distorted voice.

Arthur shook his head. *The ocean monster… can actually speak and I can't?!*

"SPEAK UP!" the ocean monster yelled at him with his scary voice.

Arthur tried to speak up words but only bubbles were coming out of his mouth.

"What are you hiding under your shirt? It's around your neck, I feel no good about it. SHOW IT TO ME NOW!" the ocean monster commanded.

With a trembling hand, Arthur pulled down the collar of his shirt and a strong light started to glow from the stone. Arthur closed his eyes; the light was too radiating. The ocean monster made very loud noises. Arthur didn't know what was happening to ocean monster, as he still couldn't open his eyes. He kept them shut tightly, he was afraid he'd go blind if he'd try to blink his eyes open. There was a whirlpool happening but not as strong as the one before. And slowly, slowly, the water calmed down.

Everything became dark and black.

There was silence!

A deep silence.

After a while, Arthur managed to open his eyes. He saw a ceiling. "Where… am I?" Arthur mumbled. Arthur could barely breathe and his stomach hurt. *I think I'll vomit.* He got up with the little strength that he had left in him and picked up the bucket that was near the bed and threw up.

"Arthur… Arthur, you're awake. Thank you Lord!" his mother said while pulling the curtains open.

How did I come back? Was I dreaming the whole time?

His mother poured water in her hand from the jug and washed his forehead. And she held his head while he was throwing up.

"It's okay, son, you'll be fine," his mother comforted him.

He stopped vomiting but his belly still hurt too much; it felt like he was nearly going to throw up his stomach off of him.

His mother helped him to lie down and covered him with a blanket. He realized then that he was actually in Ritz clinic.

"Mother, how did I get here?" Arthur slowly spoke.

"I was told a fisherman found you and brought you here. I didn't see him but that is what I was told," his mother said.

"How…? I don't get it." he inhaled deeply and tried to breathe naturally. He was thinking and said, "Have my friends arrive yet? What happened?"

"Hun, don't think too much and don't talk. Just rest, son. Everything's going to be alright," his mother said.

"But..."

And Doctor Ritz cleared his throat then pulled the curtains open.

"How are you feeling, Arthur? Tell me, anything hurts you?" the doctor asked.

"I have a headache and my stomach hurts a lot... My hand hurts me," Arthur said and he looked at his hand and three of his fingers were already wrapped.

"Yes, you broke your fingers. You shouldn't try to take this splint off. It'd take time to heal," the doctor said.

Arthur began to remember that someone stepped on his hand and he fell off... *So, that was real. I wasn't dreaming again. I wonder who was that person and why would he do that to me...? I have seen those boots before but... It can't be him...*

"Arthur... Arthur, can you hear me?" the doctor asked.

"Yes, sorry..." Arthur replied.

"Anything else hurt you?" the doctor asked.

"I'm exhausted and that's all, I think."

"He's having trouble with breathing too, Doctor," his mother said.

"Yes, I noticed that but don't worry, it's normal due to the situation that he was drowning. Excuse me, ma'am, I'll do a regular check-up for your son," said the doctor.

Arthur's mother nodded her head and said, "I'll be waiting outside, okay, son?"

The doctor did the check up, he opened Arthur's eye widely and looked carefully at it; then he did the same to his other eye. He asked him to stick his tongue out. After that, he told him to inhale and exhale deeply, he felt a strong pain.

Then, he pressed on his stomach and this was where it hurt the most.

Once he was done, he called Arthur's mother in. It was nothing serious but he recommended that Arthur should only eat soups or mashed and soft foods for a week as his stomach was too weak. Also, Doctor Ritz receipted a pain reliever to calm the pain for Arthur's broken fingers. He explained that his breathing would improve with time. All he had to do was to rest a lot, should exercise breathing by taking a deep inhale and exhale and repeating it for one minute or few minutes, three times a day.

At last, he mentioned that Arthur should stay a night here at the clinic just to make sure he'd be alright.

"Doctor, I want to go home," Arthur said and tried to get up to show the doctor he was okay. However, he ended up feeling dizzy and lay down too soon. He proved himself wrong and he had to stay.

The doctor left and Arthur's mother sat down on the bed beside his legs.

"I'll go for a little while. I'll make you a soup and come back. Don't think of anything. I want you to rest meanwhile, okay?"

"Mother... the necklace," Arthur said and searched around his neck.

"I have it, son."

"Mother, it's real... I saw the ocean monster and the necklace saved me."

"I know I know... You can tell me about it later. Just rest now, son."

"Mother, I..."

"Shh… close your eyes," Arthur's mother said and she caressed his hair and his forehead.

He couldn't resist those warm and tender hands. They made him sleepy and he quickly fell asleep like a baby.

9- Sorrow

Arthur was finally home. He sometimes found himself not believing it. Nobody could blame him for that after he went through an odd situation. So, every now and then, he would make sure if he was dreaming or not.

Arthur slowly opened his eyes and he saw the ceiling of his room. He right away looked around. He saw his desk, his windows, his room's walls... He sighed with relief. *Yes, I am home.*

The day before yesterday, he had stayed at the clinic. And on yesterday's afternoon, his uncle and his mother brought him back home. He's feeling slightly better. He still felt weak and exhausted even though he had just woken up. The sun had risen already; leaving its yellow rays and trace in his room, through the windows.

His mother opened the door slowly and gently. She peeked into his room. He looked at her and she smiled widely at him. He smiled back at her too.

"Good morning, dear," his mother said and opened the door widely.

"Good morning, Mother."

"You are awake. Why didn't you call me?"

"I just woke up. Not long time ago, and also I didn't want to bother you."

"Shh... Don't say such things. Give me your hand, let me help."

"No... No need, I can get up by myself."

"No, let me help..." His mother took his arm and put it around her shoulders but the noise of the door interrupted her.

Someone was knocking on the door loudly.

Arthur's mother's facial expression was of surprise and worry. She wasn't expecting visitors this morning. She left his room and went to open the door.

A woman started to shout at his mother. Arthur got up from his bed quickly and the world started to spin around him. He forced himself to take a step and walk. He felt dizzier and he fell down on his knees. The shouting made it all worse... He was worried that someone would hurt his mother and he couldn't do anything.

He crawled and he kept his head down. He reached the door and he was breathless. He stopped, trying to breathe. Meanwhile, he heard this woman yelling, "It's your son's fault... He is responsible for my son's death."

"Calm down, Mrs. Kenny. Let me understand what happened? Who died?" Arthur's mother said.

Arthur grabbed the knob of the door and he pulled himself up, trying to stand on his feet.

"Robert! Robert! Your son is surely the reason for his death!" Mrs. Kenny yelled.

"Robert... T-This... This can't be possible," Arthur stammered.

He sat down on the floor. He couldn't stand up and he was shocked by the news. He placed his hand on his chest. He felt suffocated to the point that everything around him became hazy and the air became heavy. *How… did he die?* His eyes felt like burning and poured hot tears. He sat there… Uselessly.

"Mother, stop!"

This is Kevin's voice.

"Mother! Arthur didn't do anything to hurt Robert. Mother, you have to accept the fact that he just drowned! And we were late to save him," Kevin said.

"Be quiet, Kevin! How come Arthur is alive and Robert isn't? Didn't they both drown in the same ocean, in the same water…? Why would they fall down in the ocean at the same time? He pushed him off! I know it! Arthur pushed my son off! My husband never liked his father. I couldn't stop this friendship that my son had with Arthur. I couldn't stop it. I wish I did something to prevent it," Mrs. Kenny yelled.

"Mother! Robert… Mother, Robert… He was the one who tried to murder Arthur… Please, let us leave from here… Enough!" Kevin said loudly.

"No, my son did no harm to anyone."

"But he did, Mother. When he heard Arthur was calling for help, instead of helping him out, he stepped on Arthur's hand to let him fall off into the ocean. Not that it, he confessed about it, he spoke loudly about it himself. He was drunk and when he realized what he did to Arthur, he regretted it but it was too late. Then when he saw us, he wasn't balanced and the ship moved hard unexpectedly and he fell off. Mother, please let us leave, the shame is covering me from head to toe!"

"My son? No, shush. I know my son," Mrs. Kenny said and wept.

"Mother, give me your hand. Let's go… Let us leave from here," Kevin said.

Mrs. Kenny became quiet and they left. However, Arthur could hear people were talking near the house. Arthur's mother closed the front door and she entered Arthur's room. She saw him sitting on the floor, crying.

"Oh dear…" his mother said.

She sat on her knees and held him. She let him cry in her arms. She rubbed his back but he also felt his mother was crying too.

Minutes passed and his mother wiped the tears off her face and she wiped his tears with her soft hands. She helped him to get up and walked him to the bathroom. She waited for him outside and then, she helped him to walk again and sit down on the chair. She then went to the kitchen.

Silence found itself in the house but Arthur's mind was loud.

He crossed his arms over the table and placed his face over them. He drifted through memories he shared with Robert…

He was always a good guy and indeed a great friend. He was there when I needed him and I was there too when he needed me. We got through hard times; we had good times and little adventures. Until, he remembered the leathered boot… *I knew deeply, it belonged to him, but I convinced myself that someone else could possibly had the same boots.* Arthur rose his head and looked at his hand and his fingers in splint. *Is this the last memory I should remember of you, Robert? I just can't believe it. I am not mad at you… I just feel I am losing my mind.*

He began to remember the last conversation they had. *Robert asked me to forgive him... Was he asking for forgiveness because he was going to get rid of me? Why would he ask me for forgiveness?* Arthur wiped his tears as he heard his mother's footsteps coming toward him.

Arthur's mother placed a bowl of soup and a glass of water on the table, right in front of him. He rose his head and looked at her. Before he moved his lips to speak, his mother said,

"I know you don't feel like eating but you have to eat it, son. You need to get well."

He shook his head and said nothing.

His mother pulled a chair beside him and sat. She took his hand and held it.

"Son. Please eat the soup, you need to take your medicine. You can't take your medicine on an empty stomach." She continued to say, "I know you're brokenhearted and I am too... I know you were too close to him. He was like a brother to you."

He looked down at the soup because he needed to avoid looking in his mother's eyes, so he wouldn't cry again; however, tears failed him again.

Arthur's mother let go his hand and she wiped his tears.

"Dear... Be strong, and I'll be here for you to be strong again. Life can be rough and we need each other to keep going. Please eat... Just for me, dear," his mother said and cried too.

He nodded his head and held her hand.

"Don't cry, Mother... I'll eat," Arthur spoke.

He finally grabbed the spoon. His hand was shaking and the spoon fell down, causing the soup to splash over his shirt.

"It is okay," his mother said and got a napkin and wiped his shirt.

"Mother, it's okay. I can do it myself."

"Sorry…" his mother said with a weak voice and she wiped her tears off. "I'll bring another spoon for you."

She went and brought him a clean spoon and he started to eat. Whenever he'd swallow little bit of the soup, it felt as if he was swallowing thorns through his throat. He just didn't want to eat but he had to. Even little things, like eating… became undesirable to him.

At same time, he found it difficult to eat with his left hand. He used to eat with his right hand. He rarely used or worked with his left hand. Arthur was looking at his broken fingers. He couldn't erase the moment Robert stepped on his fingers.

He managed to eat half of the soup and stopped. He couldn't finish it all. He took his medicine and drank water over it. It helped a little bit to make this bitter taste of medicine go away.

His mother took the bowl and the glass to the kitchen. Then she came back to him.

"Do you want me to help you to go to your bedroom?"

"No, thank you. I guess I will sit here for a while. I have lied down for too long."

His mother nodded her head.

And someone knocked on the door again! Arthur's heart skipped a beat. *I can't handle another bad news. Who could this be now?*

His mother opened the door. He heard his mother was welcoming. She pulled the door wide open and Arthur finally saw who they were! It was Billy and Peter!

They entered the house and Peter walked in a fast pace toward Arthur. Arthur tried to get up and once he stood up, Peter hugged Arthur for a little while.

"I'm glad... I'm glad you're... alive," Peter said with choking voice.

"Thank you, brother. I'm glad you're too!" Arthur replied.

He let go and he wiped his tears off. Billy stepped in and hugged Arthur as well. Billy and Peter wouldn't hug Arthur on normal days, except if they didn't see each other for long time. But this time, they did because they were grieving for the loss of a good friend.

Billy let go and looked at Arthur. He looked very drawn and tired. His eyes behind the glasses looked swollen. Perhaps, he had cried all night or he didn't even sleep.

"Are you well?" Billy asked.

"Yes... Are you well?" Arthur asked him.

"Mhm," Billy answered.

"Please have a seat. Would you like some tea, Peter? Billy?" Arthur's mother asked.

"No, thank you, ma'am," Billy said.

Peter shook his head.

"What about some water? Or are you hungry? I have some soup," she asked them again.

Billy and Peter looked at each other. They looked nervous and they didn't know what to say.

"W-Water is okay," Peter finally spoke.

Billy nodded his head with agreement.

"Alright."

Billy and Peter remained silent.

This type of silence is too disturbing but at the same time, I feel we're talking too much through this silence. Our silence speaks out our heavy emotions that our mouths fail to pronounce yet. As if we are likely reading each other's mind.

Arthur's mother placed glasses of water on the table. She went to her bedroom with a hope they'd finally speak together alone.

Out of the blue, Billy cleared his throat and made a gesture toward Peter. Peter shook his head. At this point, Arthur decided to talk.

"What's going on? Is there something you want to tell me?"

"Ye-Yes," Peter said.

But he didn't add anything more.

"There's something. Something happened, Arthur… We don't know how to tell you or perhaps you heard of it… It's about Robert," Billy managed to speak about it.

"I heard…" Arthur responded.

"You heard!? What did you hear exactly?" Billy wondered.

"Robert," Arthur paused, "is dead." Arthur choked with the sentence.

Billy and Peter were shocked that he had already heard the bitter news.

"Who told you?" Peter asked.

"His mother and Kevin… Well, they came here and talked with my mother. His mother blamed me for his death and Kevin showed up. He said that R-Robert tr-tried to get rid of me," Arthur stammered.

Silence found them again for moments.

"Actually… yes, and we're shocked," Peter said.

"How? Tell me... Please, tell me, I don't get it, why would he do that to me? Tell me," Arthur's voice rose.

Peter's face started to change into blue and sweaty because of the pressure he put on them in order to make them speak about it. Peter looked away and he started to shake a little. He didn't look well. It must've been tough on him to explain the situation to Arthur. He couldn't cope with everything yet. Arthur could see it all and he began to calm him down and stopped pushing him to talk.

"I'm sorry, Peter... I-I didn't mean to push you to talk. I-I am just angry, confused, I just don't get what's going on... I'm sorry," Arthur spoke his mind out loud.

"It's okay... You have the right to know and I was... I was one of who witnessed what happened," Peter said.

"You were there? But I remember you were asleep."

"Yes, but I woke up when I heard your voice calling our names for help. Kevin got up too and we both went upstairs to the deck and..." Peter paused.

"And?"

"You had already fallen into the ocean and... And Robert was yelling... Saying, 'I didn't want to hurt you. I don't want to kill you but it was all your fault and your father... Why my father has to die and not yours. My father never liked your father either, because your father was always like a saint in the eyes of all of people. Then it's your turn, people like you better than they liked me, even Lousina, the girl I loved. Everything you do, you are the best but not me. Why? Just tell me why?' Then he started to cry. He said that he wanted you to come back. He felt sorry. Apparently, he was so drunk."

"Then what happened?" Arthur asked.

Peter took a deep breath and said, "Kevin called his name and he looked at us and the ship suddenly turned to the other side. We tripped and caught anything so we'd not fall but Robert fell off into the ocean. When the ship finally became in control, we tried to look for you and Robert but after a few minutes passed, we only saw his body... His body was floa- floating," Peter said.

They all became quiet. Arthur's mind started to create a scene in his head, seeing Robert's dead body floating in the ocean.

Arthur looked at Billy and Peter and they seemed to spaced out. They were remembering what had happened there. It was already so bad for Arthur but surely, what they had seen and witnessed was way worse than just hearing the news.

"Are you okay?" Billy asked Arthur.

Arthur looked at them as if he just opened his eyes from a nightmare. He took a deep breath.

"I guess..." Arthur responded.

"There's something else that happened..." Billy said.

"What else!?" Arthur panicked.

"Don't panic. It's... It's not like something bad, it's bad but... just listen to me, okay?" Billy told Arthur.

"Okay," Arthur said.

"When Robert fell due that the ship spinning around strongly, we all woke up and the beds, the chairs, everything fell over at each other... I got up with other people and went on the deck... Peter just told me about what happened to Robert. Suddenly, a huge monster came out of the water," Billy spoke.

"Ocean monster!?" Arthur said loudly.

"Yes. One of his eyes was injured and it was making a very loud noise. Then it went back into the ocean and it didn't show up again," Billy said.

Is it possible that the light of the stone that I was wearing in the necklace injured the ocean monster's eye? Was it that strong? If this is true, the tale of the necklace; the one that my mother sort of told me, it's actually true. I think tales are not just tales, they're reality. It is not only me that saw the ocean monster. Everyone on the ship saw it, too!

Arthur's head began to spin and he felt dizzy. He placed his hand on his head and tried avoiding eye contact.

"Look at me, your eyelids are twitching," Billy was worried.

"Don't mind them…" Arthur closed his eyes.

"You look tired, you must rest… We stayed longer than we should have," Billy said.

Peter agreed.

"No, guys… Please stay," Arthur said.

"No, you have to rest and tomorrow we'd meet," Billy told Arthur.

Peter grabbed Arthur from his arm and helped him to get up. Billy came closer and helped as well. They walked him to his bed and help him to lie down.

"You really didn't have to do that. I can walk by myself," he said while he felt ashamed.

"We know you can walk but we wanted to help," Peter responded.

"Yes, and we also need to rest after this long trip," Billy said.

"Right," Arthur said.

"Before we leave… There will be a funeral for Robert. We actually buried him in Shellia but his family wants to have a funeral here. They'll announce which day soon," Billy mentioned.

Arthur nodded his head.

Billy shook Arthur's hand and then Peter did the same.

"We will always be together, look after yourself because we need you," Peter said and those words made Arthur emotional but brought him some strength too.

"I will. Thank you, my brothers," Arthur said.

They left his room and Arthur's head ached so much as it was recalling memories that he shared with Robert.

10- Friends

It was morning already. The sun rose up a while ago and for some reason, it decided to hide behind the clouds. Arthur had his breakfast and he was just sitting on his bed.
"It is another day," he mumbled and as usual, he had woken up from seeing a nightmare. He kept seeing the ocean monster and the same nightmare of Robert drowning and he couldn't save him. He sometimes wished the night to fly by and the morning would come quickly because he didn't desire to see another nightmare. However, today was not like any day. He wasn't looking forward to getting up early; perhaps, he wasn't looking forward waking up at all.

Today was not like any other. It was windy and it was getting cloudy all of a sudden. Clouds covered up the sun and sadness covered up Arthur's heart. Even birds which used to sing beside his windows every day; seemed to flee. They perhaps couldn't dare to chirp on this day... *The day of my best friend's funeral.*

Arthur's mother prepared another suit that belonged to his father; it was a black one and she told him to wear it. Arthur still didn't wear it. He was just sitting here; waiting for any reason to happen so he would not have to go. He couldn't imagine nor handle the eyes of people when they would see him. Questioning all the time, how he had survived and Robert did not. And the real pressure would be meeting Robert's mother at the funeral. *I just want to disappear,* he thought.

His mother knocked on the door. "Arthur, are you ready? Can I come inside?"

"Come in, please."

She opened the door and looked at him… Her eyebrows rose up and her cheeks turned blood red. Arthur knew she was really angry at him before she would speak a word. He began to apologize beforehand.

"Mother, I'm sorry but… I-I cannot…"

His mother interrupted him.

"No… Don't give me any excuses. You're going to wear the suit and going to pay respect and honor for your brother."

"Mother… I—"

"Don't say anything…" she raised her voice.

She took a few steps toward him and bent down. Her face was close to his and on the same level. Her hazel eyes were looking in his brown eyes.

"You did not do anything wrong. If you stay here and hide, you prove to the people that you did something wrong and the real shame is that you'd not go to your dear friend's funeral. Despite what he did at the end… He had a good soul. People change sometimes due to circumstances but the true soul doesn't change. I know he'd have regretted it badly and I'm sure he'd admit that he tried to hurt you and he'd go to surrender himself if he was still with us but… he's gone."

She continued to say but in a quiet voice now, "Son, get up and wipe your tears. You are now facing the real life, and life needs a brave heart."

He wiped off his tears and he nodded his head. His mother stood still and then sat down beside him. She caressed his hair and he turned his face to look at her. She kissed his shoulder and she looked at him again with tearful eyes.

"I thank God for keeping you safe every day. God knows how Mrs. Kenny feels like… We must be there for her and her family, right?" his mother said.

"Y-yes," he replied.

She nodded her head and hugged him for a while.

Once she let go, she wiped off her tears. "Alright. Get changed, okay? Your uncle is coming in any minute."

"I will."

She left his room. Arthur's mind returned to its senses. *How did I think of not going to the funeral? I shouldn't have thought of it twice… The worse thing, I did wish to be gone. How can I possibly think that way? I should look after my mother. I must be here. My mother needs me as much as I need her. Gosh… my mother is always right. I'm blessed to have a wise mother like her. Without her, I'd not understand life… I'd be a fool just like how I was a few minutes ago.*

He was barely able to wear the suit; it was pretty difficult to wear it with an injured hand. His fingers were taking so much time to heal and his body hadn't strengthened up totally yet. He could walk by himself now, but sometimes he'd feel a little dizzy and need to sit down and rest.

Arthur could hear his uncle and wife had just come over, they were chattering in the living room. They were talking about food and Charlie started to cry. Arthur's uncle opened Arthur's bedroom door; as usual, he wouldn't knock on the door first. He had such a habit. Thankfully, Arthur was fully dressed up already.

"My nephew, look what I brought you," his uncle said.

He handed him a walking cane. It was a black wooden stick, glazed with shiny paint; it looked awesome but Arthur didn't see the need for it.

"Oh, why?"

"We are going to walk to Mrs. Kenny's house and it is not nearby, you know. You would need it."

Arthur's mother entered the room and she was surprised.

"Why did you give Arthur a stick?" she asked.

"I believe, it would help him. I couldn't rent a carriage. All were rented, today unexpectedly. So, I figured to buy my nephew a walking cane to help him," Arthur's uncle replied.

"And are you comfortable to walk with it?" she asked Arthur.

"I don't know. I think people will look at me. I think I'll manage walking without it," Arthur said.

"That's what I thought," his mother said.

"It looks cool though," Arthur said.

"So, you're not going to use it?" Arthur's uncle asked. "If you feel ashamed to walk with it, I can take it in my hand and once you need, I'll give it to you."

"That sounds like a good idea," Arthur said.

"Looks like it's settled. I will go to the kitchen. Got stuff to do," Arthur's mother said and left the room.

Arthur's aunt (his uncle's wife) entered his room, she was carrying Charlie.

"How are you, Arthur?" she asked.

"I'm alright, I guess."

"Oh, you'll get better, dear." She continued to say, "Tryess, here, take Charlie; I need to help Medlee in the kitchen. I'm sure Arthur would like the company of you two," she said.

"Gosh, come here, boy. See, he stopped crying. He likes his father better," Arthur's uncle said.

"Jeez, don't get me started," his wife said and she placed her hands on her waist.

"Oh oh, please don't. I was only joking, hun," he said and laughed.

She calmed down and laughed it off as she left the room.

"Come on, Arthur, try the stick. I thought to bring you a crutch but thought it'd be difficult for you to use and it was also unnecessary. You're getting better already."

"True. Well, I'll try it now."

He took a few steps with the walking cane in his hand, he walked around the living room and back to his room. Arthur's uncle was tickling Charlie and blowing air on his belly. Charlie giggled, he seemed to like being tickled. Arthur looked at them and finally he smiled a little after it had been a while.

After half an hour passed, everyone was ready to go; Arthur's mother and uncle carried some food that she made. Charlie was just asleep in his mother's arms. This was Arthur's first time to leave the house ever since he came back home. He felt like he was seeing the town for the first time, finding a few changes that had happened but those changes might not be considered as new because he probably didn't pay attention to them before.

The good thing was that Arthur was breathing better. He was not quite breathless when he arrived to the Kennys' house and he didn't need the stick. Many people were there, giving their honest condolences to the family and shortly they'd leave; and some would stay. Arthur's mother and uncle went to ask kindly to go to the kitchen, in order to give the food there. While Arthur and his uncle's wife went inside to condole.

Arthur was not quite familiar with all of the family. He only knew Kevin and Mrs. Kenny here. He condoled everyone easily but once he reached Robert's mother, the atmosphere turned heavy. Arthur was sweating and his heart was pounding. He tried to remember what his mother told him earlier in the morning and somehow, it brought him confidence.

"I'm sorry, ma'am. My honest condolences to you and your family."

"Thank you…" Mrs. Kenny said while avoiding looking at Arthur.

Kevin was standing right next to her and Arthur said the exact words to him.

"Thank you, Arthur. It's good to see you able to go out and in a better health," Kevin said.

"Thank you, Kevin. Yes, I'm getting better…"

"Kevin, people are waiting to condole us. There's no time for talking," Mrs. Kenny said.

I understand she still cannot stand my existence and she cannot wait for me to leave. I have to be understandable… I hope one day, she'll treat me and my mother better.

"I'll catch up with you later," Arthur said.

Kevin agreed.

After Arthur was done, he looked around, trying to find empty seats to sit. He saw Billy and Peter were sitting on the other side of the room, he hadn't noticed them earlier. Billy waved at him to sit next to them. He went toward them and sat near to Billy after he greeted them both and also offered his condolence to them. Arthur's aunt also sat near Arthur and Charlie had no idea where he was, he looked around and he was falling asleep again slowly. After a while, Arthur's mother and uncle came and sat on the other seats which were in front of Arthur and his friends.

"Sorry, I didn't see you yesterday," Billy told Arthur.

"Oh no, I am the one who has to be sorry, Arthur. I didn't see you for like three days. I got busy with work," Peter said.

"Don't worry, guys. I understand. We're here now together, that can be more than enough," Arthur told them.

"That's right," Billy said.

"Are you feeling better?" Peter asked.

"Yes, kind of. I'm looking forward to when I'd be well. So I can go back to work. I want to distract myself… you know. I think working would help me with that," Arthur said.

"Yes, you'll get better and… eventually, things also will be okay again. It's tough but it shall pass," Billy said.

"I hope…" Arthur paused then said, "I just don't know if this heaviness in my chest would ever leave."

"We all feel it, Arthur…" Billy said and sighed.

"Arthur, we have each other, remember that! We're all going through the same and we should get out of it together too," Peter spoke.

Arthur nodded his head.

"Also, Robert is still with us… We don't see him anymore but I believe he's with us. I feel it," Billy said.

"I'll try to think of it that way. Guys… Your words really comfort me, thank you so much," Arthur said.

"You're welcome," Billy said and Peter nodded his head.

People were coming and leaving, it continued this way for an hour. The lunchtime was near; Arthur's mother and some other women went inside the kitchen to serve food. Mrs. Kenny followed them. Arthur's heart tensed that something was going to happen when he saw Robert's mother was following them. He excused himself and went toward the kitchen. Mrs. Kenny's voice could be clearly heard in the aisle. He stood near the door and leaned over the wall to rest himself while standing. Mrs. Kenny was speaking with Arthur's mother with a sharp tone. She was telling her there was no need for her coming and even her food. She kept saying a lot of rude things and Arthur decided to walk in… and to take his mother home with him.

But just a second before he did, his mother spoke up for herself. Arthur's mother told her just some sentences and Mrs. Kenny started to weep. "Your son is like my son. Your sadness is mine. Put the conflict that was between my husband and yours aside. Remember how close we were… You were my shoulder that I leaned on to cry and I was there for you too during the bad times. We were friends before our sons came to this world. We were friends before I met Edward and before you met Richard. I am here for you now. Let me be here… Let me feel I was your friend for once, for God's sake. Please…"

Mrs. Kenny hugged Arthur's mother and everything came to peace.

I am surprised of what I just heard. I never knew that my mother was friends with Mrs. Kenny. I don't remember they sat together and chatted someday. All I can recall is they used to greet each other kindly. It's too touching to see everything's starting to be back as normal.

He walked away before anyone noticed him being there and he sat again with his friends. Shortly after, they served the lunch and everyone ate. And said a prayer for Robert and his family.

Arthur started to feel tired; he really needed to take his medicine and lie down or even take a nap. Arthur's uncle was just about to leave because Charlie woke up some minutes ago and wouldn't stop crying. Probably he was hungry or needed to get changed. Arthur asked his mother to go home with him but she insisted to stay here and help until the evening and she told him to go with his uncle, since their house wasn't too far from Mrs. Kenny's house. He didn't have much of a choice and he accepted going to his uncle's house. He said goodbye to Billy, Peter, and Kevin. Right before he left, he saw Mrs. Kenny around and he said goodbye to her. She placed her hand on Arthur's shoulder and thanked him for coming here today. This cheered his broken heart a little bit. He felt emotional and he felt better about himself.

Then, he left with his uncle and aunt and Charlie. Arthur, at this point, was tired and he took the walking cane from his uncle and used it.

They walked for a while and arrived after some minutes. Arthur's aunt prepared the bed for Arthur in their guest room. He thanked her kindly and once she was done; he lay down and tried to nap. His mind was loud and it was hard for him to sleep but eventually, he fell asleep as his body was exhausted.

11- Looking Forward to Better Days

Arthur hated waiting, and the worse part of it was that he didn't know for how long he had to wait. He was too excited today; the doctor would remove the splints. However, he excused himself to see another patient. Arthur was trying to understand, there was another person who was much more in need to see the doctor than him but it was tough.

While he was waiting, he observed every little detail in Doctor Ritz's office out of boredom. There were three pens on the desk, four folders, and a cup of hot water that seemed to be cold now. There was no steam coming out of the cup anymore. The curtains were open and the sun light was happily wandering inside the room. The doctor's chair was left at a certain angle as he got up, he didn't push it back inside. The sunlight was dancing on the floor around the chair and Arthur imagined to watch the performance. *I think I am starting to lose my mind.* He got up and walked around in the office.

I already made a list of what I am going to do once the splints would be removed. I'd write about what I have been through lately. I'd go back to work and earn some money. It's not nice to see my mother working a lot these days. Lately, she has been baking cakes and biscuits and selling them to people, beside sewing dresses. There's no shame in working but I just want my mother to be resting and relaxing. She shouldn't worry about money while I am here. I even tried to give her some money that I saved but she refused.

Arthur's mother had said to him, "You might need them and it is your money that you were saving. When you work, it's okay, you can give me money if you like."

Thought after thought, Arthur finally sat down. And someone opened the door slowly and in a sneaky way. Arthur tried not to look but his curiosity would kill him if he didn't look. He looked at the door as it was opening and Mrs. Ritz looked at him and giggled.

"Oh, good morning, Doctor Byron," Mrs. Ritz joked with him.

She entered the office while she had a teapot and a small towel in her hand.

"Good morning, ma'am," he smiled.

"How are you, Arthur?" Mrs. Ritz asked.

She grabbed the cup and threw the water on a plant that was near the door.

"I'm well, Mrs. Ritz. Thank you for asking. How do you do?"

She put the cup back on the desk and poured some tea, she placed the small towel on the desk and put the teapot over it and she finally sat in the doctor's chair.

"Oh, you're feeling well; why are you here? And I'm doing great, thank you, Arthur," Mrs. Ritz said.

"I'm here to have my splints removed."

"Oh pfft, I was joking with you. I know why you're here. Why are you always so serious?"

"I-I don't know… This is how I am, I guess." He rubbed his hair.

"I remember you from the class before, I would make jokes and you would just shyly smile. Do you ever laugh?"

"Of course, I do!"

"I know, you do! Gotcha, I was joking with you again." She giggled.

Arthur laughed along with her. Soon enough, they became silent.

"Argh, schools are out, you know…" Mrs. Ritz broke silence. "I come here to the clinic to help my husband but he doesn't need my help but I always try to find something to do. Like making tea. Oh, would you like some tea, dear?"

"No, thank you, ma'am."

"Why?! You think teachers can't make good tea?"

"No… No, I didn't mean it that way. Today's weather is too warm and I would rather drink something cool and refreshing."

"Oh, young people prefer cool drinks in a weather like this but we adult people like to drink tea even if it'd be hot summer."

Someone knocked the door and opened it. It was Doctor Ritz.

"Sorry for keeping you waiting, Arthur," Doctor Ritz said. Mrs. Ritz got up.

"Here's your tea. Drink it up before it cools down," Mrs. Ritz said.

"Thank you, darling," Doctor Ritz said to his wife.

"I'll take my leave now. I don't want to see medical stuff happening now. It was good to see you, Arthur, and take care of yourself, okay dear?" Mrs. Ritz said.

"Thank you, ma'am."

"You need anything else, darling?" Mrs. Ritz asked her husband.

"No, thank you," Doctor Ritz replied.

"Alright, bye for now," Mrs. Ritz said.

She left the office. Doctor Ritz brought the equipment that was needed to cut off the splint. *After all the excitement that I had in me, it all has turned into stress and nervousness. He kept telling me not to move and whenever he told me so, I moved a little bit and when he didn't tell me to, I held still. However, he managed to cut them off and my fingers are finally released!*

"How does your hand feel now? Does it hurt you?" Doctor Ritz asked while wiping off the sweat from his forehead.

"No, it doesn't hurt me but it feels numb."

"Don't be afraid, move your fingers," Doctor Ritz told him.

Arthur was afraid a little bit to move his hand. His hand was shaking but not sure if it was because he was nervous or it was the way it was. He finally moved his fingers slowly. The doctor told him to open and close his hand. He did exactly what he asked him to do. His fingers did not hurt him anymore, just sort of felt weird but there was not much pain. Arthur was thrilled!

Doctor Ritz advised Arthur to open and close his hand as practice for it to get stronger ten times twice a day until his hand would feel as normal as it used to be. He also mentioned to him that he shouldn't carry heavy things right away; he had to wait for another month or two at least.

Arthur thanked the doctor kindly and the doctor took a sip of the tea and spitted it out. "Jeez, it's cold again," he poured the tea on the same plant that was near the door.

The doctor looked at Arthur awkwardly then said, "Arthur, don't tell my wife what you just saw!"

"I won't!"

He chuckled and Arthur laughed along with him. He thanked the doctor again and he left.

While he was on his way back home, Arthur was wondering whether his mother would be home or still out selling her cakes in the neighborhood.

I am really impatient to show her that my hand is better than ever! he thought as he walked home.

He looked at his hand while walking. And out of the blue, Arthur heard a bicycle bell ringing behind him. He moved aside but that person wouldn't stop ringing the bell.

"Jeez, who's this person?!" Arthur mumbled and he turned around to look at the annoying person.

"It's you! Why are you being so noisy?"

Peter laughed out loud.

"Is this how you greet your friend? You didn't even say hello… Look at you, your face is red like a tomato sauce," Peter said.

Arthur sighed and shook his head.

"Hi, Peter."

"Hey! Come on, bud. Chill out. Did you notice something new? Look at me."

Arthur looked at him. He noticed nothing new about him. He had seen him wearing this hat, this shirt before, also the trousers, and the shoes.

Peter rang the bell of his bike again.

"A bicycle!?" Arthur said.

"Gosh, takes you forever to notice it. And before you tell me, I'm glad your hand is fine now," Peter said.

"Oh, you noticed? I don't know how I didn't recognize your bicycle right away…"

"Ah, don't worry about it. Perhaps it's because I got you angry a tiny bit. I don't think too well when I get mad either," Peter said.

"That could be the reason… Hey, will you let me to try it sometime?"

"You can try it now but is your hand well enough?"

"I guess." Arthur was still a little afraid to use his hand. "Well, let it be for next time."

Peter got off his bike and pulled it alongside him as he walked with Arthur.

"You're going home?" Peter asked.

"Yes, I am. You can come with me, if you like."

"I'd like to but how about we go out instead? Also get to meet Billy too, what you say?" Peter suggested.

"That sounds great but I have to stop by and see my mother first."

"Sure thing, I will wait for you outside."

"Okay, I won't take long."

Arthur went inside his home and the whole house smelled like vanilla cake! He saw his mother was in the kitchen. Once she saw him, her eyes sparkled with happiness as if she had seen him after a long time. She was happy that his hand had gotten better.

She hugged him and told him that she was too glad that his hand was alright now and she told him not to work right away. Arthur didn't know how she could always read his mind; he was actually planning to start working tomorrow. He couldn't risk losing another job. Mr. Jones had hired someone else; he couldn't wait for Arthur to get well... that really disappointed him. At least, he still had his job at Lomar's leather shop. Mr. Lomar was kind enough and he offered a full job for Arthur. Of course, Arthur said yes right away. But he wasn't sure if he would let him have a longer vacation.

I hope Peter's father wouldn't mind giving me extra couple of days off. I guess, my mother is right. The doctor told me to not carry heavy stuff and to be careful. I personally am a little worried to carry something with it yet.

"Well, Mother. I will go out for some time with Peter and Billy. Actually, Peter is waiting for me outside."

"Shame, shame. How many times have I told you to let your friends in?"

"I did tell him, don't worry. He just wanted to go out and probably he didn't want to leave his bicycle outside."

"He got a bicycle? That's a good thing. Maybe one day, you save up money and buy one for yourself."

"Yeah, maybe."

"It's alright, son, let's not let Peter wait longer for you. Have fun."

"Thanks, Mother."

Peter was riding his bicycle back and forth… He had all the right to show off; he was one of the few who had bikes in Tulipia. Arthur called him and he stopped his showing off around. He asked Arthur if he'd like to sit behind him because he didn't feel like walking and pulling his bicycle at the same time. Arthur told him that he'd like to walk and he didn't mind Peter riding the bicycle. Peter rode his bike slowly ahead of Arthur.

Before they reached Billy's house, they came near Robert's house. Arthur's feet stopped and his heart got pinched. He remembered how they used to stop by to take Robert with them before going to Billy. Peter stopped and looked at Arthur.

"I know how it feels… He's with us, never forget that. Come on… Let's go," Peter said and smiled a broken smile.

"R-right…"

Then they got to Billy's house but he was not there. His mother told them that he was at the jewelry shop. He was staying there because his father was out of town.

"You know what, I'm going to sit behind you. It seems like I'd be walking longer now."

"Finally, you accepted. I hope you're not going to be heavy."

Arthur sat behind him.

"Oh, don't complain after you offered to pick me up with your bike."

"Yes, sir!" Peter responded.

And they went to Billy at the shop. They greeted him and he was happy to see Arthur's hand without splints. Then they asked him if he could go somewhere with them. He accepted right away and closed the shop.

Arthur walked with Billy.

"Congrats on your new bike."

"Thank you! I've been saving up for it. I figured I'd rather buy a bicycle than buy a horse."

"Imagine Peter riding a horse," Arthur chuckled.

"How is he going to climb it first?" Billy joked and laughed.

"Hey, guys, I am not that short and come on, I can ride a horse, I mean probably. Anyways, I am fine with my height," Peter spoke up for himself.

"Oh, come on, we're joking with you. And yes, your height is good. Actually, bicycles are becoming a big deal now. People have kind of lost interest in horses," Arthur said.

"That's true," Billy agreed then said, "but, Peter, you probably would get taller."

"No way, I just turned 18," Peter said.

"Some people still get taller until the age of 20," Billy explained.

"Let's hope that is not true. If it is, then that means you're going to be way taller and hard to reach," Peter mocked Billy.

"I don't mind, then I wouldn't have to climb a tree like you to pick a fruit," Billy teased Peter.

"Oh, hey, don't make fun of me now," Peter said.

"You started it, therefore, you got to handle it," Billy replied.

"No, you started it with saying that I can't get on a horse. Arthur, say something. Get on my side," Peter spoke.

"Please don't involve me into this. Where are we going anyway?" Arthur responded.

"Oh right, to the beach!" Peter said.

"Are we going to ask the people again?" Billy wondered.

Lately, Arthur and his friends had been asking the fishermen at the port and on the beach if they knew who had saved Arthur's life. Arthur wanted to know so badly. Unfortunately, nobody knew… They only gave this same answer, "It could be a fisherman from another island or country," and nobody knew him. At this point, Arthur gave up.

"No, I don't want to ask no more," Arthur said.

"Yes, please don't let us ask people. Just appreciate you're alive, bud. Let us have fun and relax," Peter said.

"Yes!" Arthur said.

"Alright then, to the beach we go!" Billy was excited about going there.

12- Questions and Commands

It was a very sunny day, a bit windy but it was warm; the perfect time for a picnic or for swimming. The waves sounded like music for Arthur and the seagulls sounded like singers. And he never got bored of listening to them.

Summer would be nice if the weather would remain this way. July was on the way and this weather would turn to be really hot. Arthur disliked summer even though he was born in it; he just hated to sweat all day long. And on the other hand, Lillianta's winter was too cold. Arthur was glad that there were Spring and Autumn in between; they were surely his favorites.

Arthur took off his shoes and walked on soft and ticklish sand. It felt refreshing and relaxing at the same time. Peter carried his bicycle and Billy helped him too. It was not a good idea to take a new bicycle to the beach where the shore's sand and carves wouldn't accept to be flat.

"Guys, we should have planned for going to the beach earlier... Look how beautiful the beach is, I really want to swim," Billy said while observing the blue sea.

"Wow, I am thinking the same thing," Arthur agreed.

"Well, looks like we all have the same thought. Why don't we just swim anyway?" Peter suggested.

"No way, I can't go back home with soaking clothes" Arthur said.

"Arthur is out of it. What about you, Billy?" Peter asked.

"No, we can swim on the next weekend though. What do you think?" Billy demanded.

"Eh, you both don't have a sense of adventure anymore," Peter said.

Peter put his bicycle down. Sat down with a frowning expression on his face. Billy and Arthur sat with him.

"Pfft, now what?" Peter said.

"Seems like I'm not the only one who gets tensed quickly," Arthur mumbled.

"I heard you," Peter said.

"Guys, let's relax now. Why don't we talk about something…? Just enjoy," Billy told them.

"You start, find us a topic to talk about," Peter replied.

"I don't know why you always choose me to find a topic but alright. I'd give you suggestions this time though," Billy said.

"Looks like you were waiting for this moment a long time and you're well prepared. Go ahead," Peter said while lying down on his side.

"Since we're on the beach away from people, we can talk about personal stuff or test our courage?" Billy told them.

"What do you mean? Are we going to play a game?" Arthur asked.

"Yes, questions or commands!" Billy said.

"Oh, this is exciting, I want to go first," Peter quickly sat on his knees with excitement.

"Wait, this is not how the game works. We have to spin a bottle," Billy replied.

"We don't have a bottle," Arthur said.

"Right… What about scissor-paper-rock?" Billy suggested.

"You're always a genius, let's do it!" Peter liked the suggestion.

This game will get me on my nerves because I don't know what I am going to expect… Neither what type of questions nor commands, Arthur thought to himself.

Billy asked them if they were ready and both Arthur and Peter nodded their heads. They played scissor-paper-rock and Arthur went with rock. Luckily, Billy and Peter went for scissor.

"Gosh, no… again, please again," Peter couldn't accept his first defeat.

"No. Arthur, go on. Who you're going to choose first?" Billy asked.

"Wait, isn't he supposed to ask both of us?" Peter wondered.

"Yes, both of us lost. Actually, it's up to you," Billy said.

"Alright… I think… I'd like to ask each of you, so each of you has their own time to answer. I guess I will pick Peter first to answer," Arthur said.

"I knew it, I wish I had gone with paper but I'd also lose because Billy chose scissor," Peter vented.

"Stop complaining, I will go easy with you. Questions or commands?" Arthur asked.

"Questions!" Peter answered.

"Billy?" Arthur asked.

"Questions too," Billy answered.

Arthur told them to wait for him to think of a question and Arthur was not very creative at asking questions, neither giving commands. *I remember Peter mentioned before that he'd like to find a beautiful girl and marry her, something like that… When Billy asked us what we would do if we'd found ourselves on an island that we didn't know.*

I'll decide to ask him if he's in love or ever been in love.

"Alright, Peter… Are you in love or have you ever been in love?" Arthur asked.

Peter chuckled. "What kind of question is this?" Peter said and his blushing cheeks could tell something.

"Come on, answer it," Billy said.

"Well, yes… I mean, well… what a stupid question, bud. Don't ask questions like that," Peter responded.

"Why are you so secretive about it? Tell us who she is," Billy said.

"This is uncomfortable, guys," Peter chuckled again and continued to say. "It's just that… The truth is, she doesn't know that I like her but I think she likes me… Forget it, it's complicated," Peter said.

"Explain…" Billy said.

"Yes, come on, Peter," Arthur said.

"Okay, okay, don't be too pushy. It is nothing. You know the other day; Arthur and I went to the shops… because he wanted me to help to carry flour and such. I saw a beautiful girl with long curly hair. She looked at me; at first, I thought she was looking at Arthur because you know, girls are always into brunet or blond guys. He's brunet and I am not. Anyways, when I turned my face to look at Arthur, I didn't see him. He was already inside the shop. I looked back at her and I pointed at myself. Wondering if she was looking at me. She giggled shyly and walked away," Peter spoke about it.

Billy and Arthur laughed out loud. They just could not hold it back!

"Stop laughing at me… I won't tell you anything again!" Peter spoke loudly.

His face was too red, he was probably burning inside like a fire. *I hope he wouldn't end up beating us,* Arthur chuckled as he thought of it.

"Easy…" Arthur said and laughed. "Easy… but why did you point at yourself?" Arthur asked.

"Yes, exactly why?" Billy said and burst into laughter again.

"Guys, if you don't stop it, I will leave!" Peter spoke seriously.

They tried their best to stop laughing.

"I'm sorry," Arthur said and he tried his best to have a serious expression on his face.

"I'm sorry too. Just curious, why do you think girls only like guys with brown or blond hair?" Billy wondered.

"Come on, man. Look at us, you and me have black hair and barely someone looks at us. They always looked at Arthur and Robert," Peter explained.

"Not really, girls have different tastes. Actually, can I answer this question or you have a different question for me?" Billy asked Arthur.

"You can answer it, if you want. I didn't come up with a question for you yet," Arthur responded.

"Alright, I will answer it. Well, I am in love with a girl. See, it doesn't deal with the color of the hair."

"Wait, what? You're in love? Who is she?" Peter's face was full of surprise.

"She is from Serina. I met her there when I was seeing the doctor. Her name is Lilly, next year she will continue her higher studies. That's why I took a year break in order to join her," Billy explained.

Arthur thought about love… *I have never fallen in love. I wonder how it feels like. How did Billy know he's in love with Lilly or how did Peter know he had feelings for that girl he saw the other day? Does love come from a look in the eyes? It sounds unrealistic but I shouldn't judge it since I have never felt it.*

"Wow! All that was happening and we never knew… Wait, you don't look surprised, Arthur, you knew about it!?" Peter said while pushing Arthur.

"What?" Arthur became present again.

"Hello! How can you be absent-minded this quick? Did you know that Billy likes a girl named Lilly?" Peter asked.

"Ah… yes, I did," Arthur answered.

"I am very disappointed now," Peter said and crossed his arms.

"I didn't tell you because I knew you would laugh at me but surprisingly you didn't. I am sorry, from now on… I won't keep something from you," Billy said.

"Yeah… Yeah, I will try to believe it. Let's continue to play the game. Ready? Scissor-Paper-Rock!" Peter said.

This time Arthur went with paper and he lost with Billy. Peter won this time with scissor, this was karma indeed! Peter was filled of excitement and happiness again as if he had won the lottery.

I am sure he'd ask us really personal questions or would order us to do something embarrassing, Arthur thought.

"My turn to get you both all at once, ready? Questions or commands, folks!" Peter stood up.

"Questions," Arthur answered.

"Commands," Billy answered.

"Guys, you should choose the same. I am not smart enough to come up with a command and a question at same time," Peter said.

"Arthur, say commands," Billy demanded.

"No… I don't want to," Arthur said.

"Listen to Billy, choose commands… You have to, it's my revenge," Peter spoke.

"You sound scary now," Arthur chuckled.

"You should be scared!" Peter said.

"Have some courage in yourself, Arthur, go for it," Billy encouraged Arthur.

"Fine, commands!" Arthur said.

"Great then," Peter said.

Peter took off his shirt.

"What are you doing?" Arthur asked Peter.

He took off his belt.

"Hey, don't strip down in front of us" Billy said loudly.

"Oh sorry," Peter said and turned to the other side and took off his pants.

He stayed in his shorts, "I command you both to swim with me."

He ran toward the sea and started to swim.

"Looks like we have no choice," Billy said while unbuttoning his shirt then his trousers.

Then he joined Peter.

I really don't want to go back home with soaking clothes, people will watch us. After all that, I am pretty sure that my mother will shout at me like I'm a child. I don't want all that. I will just sit down and watch them swimming. They look like they're having fun.

Peter was shouting, "The water is the best and, Arthur, you're just missing a lot of fun."

Arthur didn't respond to him. That still wouldn't get him up to go to swim.

After a while passed, Billy and Peter came up to Arthur. He asked them if they were done, so they could go home. They didn't answer him and instead of that, they both caught him and lifted him up.

"Guys, put me down… Hey, stop it!" Arthur was shouting.

"You have to…" Billy said.

Suddenly, Arthur heard gurgling sound in his ears as he was under water. He got up on his feet, the water wasn't that deep. He coughed and spitted all the water that he swallowed.

The water was quite refreshing and at this point, Arthur's clothe were wet anyway. So, he just continued swimming with them until the sun was almost to go down. They all agreed to go home before it got dark. As Arthur was walking his way out of water, something touched his foot. He freaked out! He felt a shiver going along his spine to his head.

He looked down slowly and all he could see was a bottle. He bent down to pick it up and he saw a big shell inside the bottle.

How did a huge shell get inside a bottle? he wondered.

He showed it to his friends and they were wondering if someone made a glass bottle and placed the shell inside it. Or made the glass bottle over the shell. They were confused but they only guessed this could be a decoration and nothing important since there was no letter or note inside it.

"It makes no sense to be just a decoration but I will take it with me anyway," said Arthur.

Billy and Arthur walked through the town, while Peter was enjoying his ride ahead of them. People looked at them and showed ashamed expression on their faces. Arthur was worried more about how his mother would react to him and seeing him with soaking wet clothes.

I know I'm no longer a kid but my mother wouldn't like to see me like this.

And indeed, Arthur's mother wasn't happy once he arrived home. She probably thought that Arthur didn't care but he did care… She just didn't give him the chance to explain himself.

"Jeez, you will never grow up," she complained.

"Mother, let me explain, it was a challenge so I had to…"

"Go get changed and take a bath," and she went to her bedroom to rest after a long day.

He went to his bedroom and placed the bottle that had the shell inside it on his side table that was near his bed. He went to take a bath and once he was done and got dressed, all he saw was one plate of food for him and his mother stayed in her bedroom resting.

She must be too tired, working and baking all day and I think I really upset her this time too, I should apologize again, he thought to himself.

13- The Shell Inside the Bottle

Arthur was walking on the ice with his friends, with lots of caution. The weather was foggy, and they only could see white, nothingness, and a hollowness surrounding them. Arthur and his friends tried to hold each other's arm so they wouldn't get lost in this unknown place. Arthur would call their names and make sure they were near; as if holding arms wasn't enough. They would reply to him. Until the moment when Peter's voice was gone. Arthur asked Billy if Peter was still holding him. He didn't reply. Arthur felt his arm was cold and he touched both of his arms and he realized he was going into this place by himself. All of a sudden, something pulled him from underneath... He fell, and he woke up from this nightmare.

Poor Arthur, nightmares didn't leave him during the nights. He looked around; he was just in his room. It was dark but he could see little bit from street light.

"I am in my room and I am in my bed. I was only seeing another nightmare," he mumbled to himself, trying to convince himself it was just another bad dream. He was sweating and his throat felt dry. *I think I will drink right away from the jug. I can't see where's the glass with all the things I have on the side table*, he grabbed it successfully and drank from it. He placed it back but his hand felt weak and the jug slipped out of his hand and everything on his side table fell off… making a huge breaking noise. He got up but he didn't put his feet down, he couldn't see all the broken pieces of glass. He heard his mother's steps cracking on the wooden floor as she walked fast to his room and she opened up the door. She had a candle lantern in her hand.

She looked pretty tired.

"Are you okay? What happened?" she asked and looked around.

"I'm… I'm sorry, Mother, I didn't mean to wake you up at this time. I just got thirsty and I…"

His mother placed the candle lantern on the floor and bent down to collect the pieces of glass.

"No, Mother, I will clean up."

"It's okay, I will do it. Stay in bed, you shouldn't walk barefoot."

He tried to bend over without putting his feet down. He grabbed a book, the shell, and his lantern and shook them off of the broken glass before he placed them back on his side table. The book was wet though. After his mother was done collecting the big pieces of the broken glass, she left the room and came back with a broom and his shoes.

He wore his shoes and she asked him to bring a piece of cloth from the kitchen. He went and brought two pieces of cloths. He started to wipe the water off of the floor once his mother was done sweeping the floor. Then, when he was done, he wrapped the book with the other piece of cloth, letting it dry. His room was clean and everything was okay again.

He lighted up his lantern for extra lighting.

"You should go back to sleep, there are still a few hours before the sun rises," his mother said.

He nodded his head.

"Are you okay, hun? You don't look well. Do you want me to make you a hot drink? Maybe chamomile?" his mother asked.

"I don't know... I don't know if that will help me to sleep," he said with hopeless voice.

His mother sat on his bed.

"Tell me, what is bothering you?"

"It's just another nightmare... A strange one."

"Do you want to tell me about it?"

He shrugged his shoulders.

"Was your nightmare about the ocean monster again?"

"No... It's different..."

"Don't think about it, son. Just relax and try to sleep. You have to work today. You need to get enough rest. If you decide to stay up for a little while and want to talk with me, I will be in the kitchen. I'll make chamomile tea to help me to sleep."

He nodded his head.

His mother left the room with her candle lantern. He lay down without shutting his eyes. He looked at the ceiling while thinking of the dream that he saw. His eyes were not tired and they seemed to forget how to sleep again. He decided to join his mother.

He got up and took his lantern with him. His mother was sitting and waiting for the water to boil.

"I guess, I want to talk about the dream that I saw," Arthur spoke.

"Sure, come sit," his mother said, pointing at the chair near her.

Arthur sat down and he told her all about it in detail. "The thing that bothered me the most was that I was being pulled down. Perhaps, my friends got pulled down before me too." His mother looked at him quietly while thinking. She finally spoke, "Son, it's just a dream. We sometimes see dreams that have no meanings or of something we heard of. Were you thinking about some tales you read before?"

"Tales? No, I didn't… the last time I read tales were the ones that my father owned, perhaps a few years ago."

"Have you read about Oernatus' sea. It's always foggy and sometimes it appears to be sea of white dandelions."

"No."

"No? I thought Edward had that book somewhere in the basement but it was a strange book," she shook her head. "I never liked it. It was telling much about war and strange things… But I thought I saw it with you before?"

He shrugged.

"Eh, anyways, Arthur, when it is about being pulled down or falling down, it isn't always a scary or bad thing. Like remember Sharona Desert that I told you about before?"

"Sharona Desert?"

"Yes, remember the necklace I gave to you? It has a red stone. This type of stone is only found in Sharona Desert."

"Oh yes, yes, I remember but we never continued the conversation."

"That's right. Well, the stone that was in the necklace was found in Sharona desert which is situated in far west. Those small red stones are found under the ground, I don't mean like you have to dig to find them… But you go or actually fall to under the ground," his mother explained.

"What… What do you mean like going under the ground?" Arthur asked.

"Let me continue. There are moving sands… The desert is huge and wide. However, there is that one spot where moving sands are. They're not like moving sands we read about or heard of. They're not muddy. They're dry, golden sands. It pulls the person down and usually the person dies, you know, from regular moving sands. But in Sharona desert, the moving sands don't kill the person but it takes him to another place underground where there are those unique stones to find."

"But, Mother…" Arthur rubbed his eyes to make sure he was awake. He couldn't believe that his mother had started to talk about those tales. "I mean… Okay, I believe in these tales. I mean I saw it happening in front of my eyes how the stone protected me from the ocean monster, or whatever it is called. Because I saw them. But…"

"But what?"

"People don't believe in them. And they don't speak about them."

"Naturally."

"But why?"

"Hun, actually, those tales aren't tales. They're history. And people don't talk about them. Thinking that if they do, they'd repeat history. And on the other hand, they tore and burned most of the books about them."

"They did that?"

"Yes, so nobody shall read and talk about them. That's why I told you, you shouldn't take any books or journals of your father outside the house and never speak about them.

This land has lived in peace for years now. They believe peace happened because they burned those cursed books."

"Mother, aren't you afraid of telling me about them now?"

"I am and also I am not. The reason I am telling you about them now because, look, it's almost three in the morning maybe? Nobody's awake but walls do have ears too that's why I am afraid little bit."

The tea pot began to make noise. Arthur and his mother got scared.

"It is the tea pot," she laughed and Arthur laughed too. "That was out of the blue. It scared us," his mother said.

She got up. She picked the teapot up with a piece of cloth and put it aside. She brought two cups and placed them on the table. She again picked up the teapot and poured the hot water in cups. At last, she added few of dried chamomile in both of the cups.

Arthur spaced out, thinking of what his mother had said. He was confused. He was afraid. He was frightened to the point he thought about never going to sail again or travel anywhere. He had had enough of what he saw earlier. The ocean monster. Being pulled by the whirlpool then the necklace saved him. He lost a friend. He realized the tales were all true but lately, he had started to convince himself these tales were just tales, even though he finally got to know they were not. Just like how he thought before. But even when his mother confirmed it to him, he preferred not to believe in those tales and let them be unspoken as people did, to have peace in his mind and life.

Once his mother finished drinking her chamomile tea, she broke the silence; "You're quiet now. You're sleepy?"

"I guess…"

Arthur's mother knew he didn't look that sleepy. She reached his hand and held it. "Son, I didn't mean to scare you about it, I just wanted to prove to you that some things are real... It was true I told a few of those tales as bedtime stories when you were a child and your father did write about them too or even had few rare books about them... Somehow, you need to know those things are real, especially now that you're an adult. Not everyone knows about these tales or let's refer to them as history now, okay? But as I knew about them, I could no longer keep the truth from you since you already had seen a few."

Arthur nodded his head.

"Mother... since we have spoken about them now, does that mean something will happen to us?"

"No. Don't worry," she patted his hand. "My grandfather told me lots about them and nothing happened. Alright now, you should go to bed."

"Okay."

They both got up, leaving the cups on the table. She went to her bedroom and Arthur went to his bedroom. He felt his bedroom was hot. He opened the other window.

Maybe a nice breeze would enter my room and help me to sleep again.

The dawn was soon and sun was ready to rise. Arthur fell asleep when it was dawn. He hadn't slept well, he ended up waking up again. He was mostly tired at the beginning of new days.

He got himself ready for the day. He had his breakfast, yet it was a little early for him to go. He went to his room to check his book; it hadn't dried out yet. He looked at the shell that was once inside the bottle and he smiled at the thought; *I remember I listened to a shell when I was a child and it sounded like echoes. My father told me he could hear the ocean's waves from the shell but I couldn't... Later on, when I grew up, I found a shell on the shore and I listened to it, and indeed it sounded like waves.*

He sat on his bed, grabbed the shell and placed it against his ear... A sudden freezing shiver hit his spine and his eyes opened widely. *I can't believe what I heard!*

"Oernatus needs your help," a voice echoed inside the shell.

Arthur got up... He threw the shell on his bed. "What's happening with me? I must be tired... Yes, I didn't sleep well, I might be just imagining stuff. This is not real." he spoke.

He shook his head. *What if what I heard is real...?* He walked forward and backward in his small room. *No, no, enough of this. Nobody found Oernatus anyway; rumors said that it vanished. But what if it wasn't vanished and they need our help? Wait, this book, this is the book my mother was talking about. I don't remember when I brought it to my room and I kept it here beside me the whole time. Yes, I think it was that one I read before once, I remember it was about Oernatus and the war...*

He sat down on his bed grabbing the book, and he opened it. He tried to find the pages that mentioned about Oernatus. There... There it was but the ink had smeared all over those pages and he couldn't read a single word of it. *Why did only these pages get damaged and the rest of the book is quite fine?*

Arthur gazed at the shell. *This could be just real,* he thought. He grabbed it while his hand was trembling and he listened to it again… and again. He still heard the same thing!

He put the book aside and he put the shell into his bag.

I must let Peter and Billy listen to it, I need to know if it is only me who can hear such things or not.

He left his room and said goodbye to his mother and left home quickly. His mother was confused of his attitude. He walked in a hurry… He wanted to arrive to the tannery and leather shop early. *I need to show it to Peter before we start working,* he told himself.

He indeed arrived early, and even before Mr. Lomar got here, and he looked too surprised to see Arthur this early.

"Good morning, Arthur, you're early today?" Mr. Lomar said while unlocking the door of the shop.

"Good morning, sir. Yes. Is Peter on his way?" Arthur asked.

"Probably. He was just having his breakfast when I left the house," Mr. Lomar replied.

"Oh, I see," Arthur said.

"Since you're early," Mr. Lomar opened the door of the shop, "I think I will let you help me clean the shop, okay? And also, I don't want you to work at the tannery. I like your job at making those leathered sacks, belts, and shoes. Even the customers liked them. I will let you work freely and you can come up with different ideas too," Mr. Lomar said.

"Sure thing, I'll do it," Arthur said.

"Yes, and I will let Mike and Robin be with you when they arrive. Teach them some more things, they're good but not as good as you," Mr. Lomar said.

"Thank you for your compliment, sir. I will teach them," Arthur responded.

"Good," Mr. Lomar said.

Arthur finished cleaning the shop with Mr. Lomar, and Peter hadn't arrived yet. Mike the new worker had come already and Arthur began to teach him some of the things. Once he had started showing Mike how to make a belt, Peter showed up. Arthur greeted him and he wanted to pull him aside to tell him about the shell. However, his father saw him that he came late, and got angry at him and then he told him to work in the tannery.

It seems like I have to be really patient and wait until Peter gets a break, thought Arthur.

Arthur spent hours teaching those guys how to make belts. Robin was a quick learner but Mike, not really. Robin managed to make two belts by himself but Mike was still stuck. Mr. Lomar's business was getting bigger and bigger each day, no wonder why he wanted more workers to learn more things than just work in the tannery.

They got a break; Arthur decided not to tell Peter about it. He needed to tell him about it privately and he just talked about regular things with him while eating. However, he told Peter that he needed to speak with him and Billy after work.

And the time had finally come. They finished working in late afternoon. Peter told Arthur to go ahead of him because he needed to take a bath after working most of the day at the tannery. Luckily for Arthur, he only worked in the shop.

Arthur went to Billy's house, he felt quite tired but he really wanted to tell them all about it. He knocked on the door and Billy opened the door himself.

"Hi, Billy... Sorry for coming at this time but I really wanted to meet you and Peter at the beach. Can you go with me there now?" Arthur asked.

"Hi... This sounds too serious, is everything alright though?" Billy asked.

"Yes, don't worry. Shall we go?" Arthur asked.

"Yes, let's go." Billy replied.

They walked to the beach and just sat there and waited for Peter. Billy was curious to know but he noticed that Arthur wasn't going to say anything until Peter would be here. Shortly, Peter arrived and rang his bike's bell, his hair was still wet after taking a bath. He put it aside and came to them.

"Hi, Billy, how's it going?" Peter said.

"Hi, I'm alright but too curious to know what Arthur has to say," Billy spoke.

"Oh, me too. You didn't start talking about it, did you?" Peter asked.

Arthur shook his head and he opened his bag and took the shell out.

"Billy and Peter... You two have to listen to it," Arthur said.

"What? You made us come all the way to listen to a shell. Have you lost your mind?" Peter said.

"It's not like any shell... Believe me," Arthur said.

"Man, I am going back home, I didn't even have dinner," Peter said with a temper.

"Peter, calm down. I didn't have dinner too. I didn't even go home yet to rest nor to take a warm bath. I came all the way here because it's serious, I promise," Arthur explained.

Billy grabbed the shell from Arthur's hand. He looked at Arthur and then he looked at Peter. He placed it on his ear and his face expression totally changed within seconds. His face turned into blue.

"H-how? How can a shell speak?" Billy said and stared at the shell with horror.

"What? The shell speaks? This is a joke," Peter said and took the shell from Billy's hand.

He listened to it. Arthur and Billy looked at him carefully, and there was no reaction.

"I hear nothing," Peter said.

"Listen carefully, Peter!" Billy demanded.

He rubbed his ear, perhaps his ears were a little blocked after taking bath. And listened to it. He started to jump and he threw the shell on the sand.

"This shell is cursed. This shell is cursed," Peter yelled.

"Shhh, be quiet. Now tell me what you heard?" Arthur asked.

"I heard that Oernatus is waiting for you," Billy said.

"I only heard Oernatus and I threw it away. What's Oernatus?" Peter wondered.

"It's a country… or a kingdom. We had a war against it, long years ago… you know, when they made *Maxemus* the battleship for it before," Arthur said.

"Okay… Why does it say it's waiting for you or us…? What did it say to you, Arthur? The same thing?" Peter asked.

"No, it said that Oernatus needs your help. I don't know if the shell was meant to come to Lillianta or to us or others… But it came to us. Maybe they need our help," Arthur said.

"What should we do?" Peter asked.

Arthur remained silent. He thought to himself, *I can't drag my friends into this. I have no intention of sailing the ocean again; it's enough what I have seen… I cannot let myself face horror one more time. But on second thoughts, I want to help and I believe Oernatus has many answers for me. I faced supernatural things and I saw things that I thought never existed… I've got a feeling I will see more. I admit I am not brave for this and there's no way I am going there by my own. I need Billy and Peter to come with me, since they're involved into it now. They listened to this mysterious shell, it can't be a joke or an imagination. It's real. If they're going, I am going too.*

Billy looked at Arthur and he seemed to read Arthur's mind as he understood his silence for Peter's question.

"We should go to Oernatus," Billy broke the silence.

"What? No! I am not going there, guys… Forget it." Peter shook his head.

"I have known you braver than this, Peter," Billy said.

"Look who's talking, you think you are brave enough to go there? We had a war against them before, you want to get killed, huh?" Peter spoke.

"That was ages before. We weren't even born yet and our parents weren't even born when that happened. And wait, keep in mind… Lillianta had a war 100 years ago against Rubia, and the neighboring countries. Even against Shellia. But look, we visited Rubia and Shellia, and nobody hurt us.

People don't live in the past, Peter. They need our help; you should understand this," Billy said loudly.

"Right, then we should tell the chief about this. Let him help them," Peter suggested.

"He won't," Arthur finally said.

"What do you mean?" Peter wondered.

"He won't help them. He believes that Oernatus is abandoned or it's vanished by a volcano or something. All the men of the country believe that too. It is useless. They won't help. They're glad that it's gone," Arthur said.

"We need to go there first, then once we'd be back, we could ask for their help after. We need to prove to them that Oernatus still exists," Billy suggested.

"Exactly," Arthur agreed.

Peter sighed and sat down.

"And how are you going to do that? We don't have a boat or ship. Don't tell me we're going to steal one," Peter said.

"I've got this solved before you could ask. My family has two boats; I can use one of them," Billy said.

"And what if we sail there and pirates show up?" Peter asked.

"I got a pistol and a hunting gun," Billy said.

"What?" Peter and Arthur said in shock.

"My father actually owned them. Why are you shocked? You have never gone hunting before? Well, I have," Billy replied.

"But you don't seem like you are into hunting and stuff… I mean when we watched the gladiators, you and Arthur couldn't look at them fighting," Peter said.

"That's a different thing. I hate violence; I don't like to see animals get killed for a show and a man dies to gain freedom or wealth. I would only fight or use gun to protect myself and hunting to survive but not for pleasure," Billy explained.

Peter and Arthur became silent. Not only because they were shocked by Billy but the thought of how dangerous it was to sail with a small group in the ocean. Things could happen, they possibly would get lost, pirates could show up if they still existed, the ocean monster, and more. On the positive side, there was a slight chance that nothing bad would happen and they could arrive safely there.

"Okay… I am in," Peter broke his silence.

"You are?!" Arthur said.

"Don't tell me you're backing off now, Arthur?" Peter spoke.

"No… no, I am not. However, we should plan this well first."

"I've got a plan, hear me out carefully," Billy explained. "This Saturday, we're going to Shellia and from Shellia, we're going to Oernatus. We tell our families we're going to Shellia for the weekend."

"Why this Saturday…? Isn't that soon? Let it be for next Saturday," Peter interrupted Billy.

"This Saturday or next Saturday… Does it make any difference?" Billy wondered.

"I don't know," Peter said.

"You're just making excuses. Let me continue," Billy spoke.

Peter sighed.

"We'll go by my boat. I can't take my family boat. It's bigger but I can't take it without their knowing. However, I will take the hunting shotgun and a pistol without telling them. Don't worry, I've got a feeling we won't have to use them but we will keep them with us for our safety. It's better to leave in early morning or at dawn," Billy suggested.

"I think it's better at dawn," Arthur said.

"Why?" Peter asked.

"I am – I am not going to tell my mother about this trip," Arthur said.

"What do you mean? Have you lost your mind!?" Billy asked.

"I can't lie to my mother again. I promised her that I will never lie to her after we went to Rubia. This is my own situation… You don't have to do the same thing like me. I will just leave without telling her. I perhaps will leave a letter for her to read so she doesn't get worried," Arthur said.

"You're crazy," Peter said.

Billy sighed. "Are you sure you won't tell her? Is this your last decision?" Billy asked.

"Yes. Yes, this is it," Arthur replied.

"Are we going to meet at the port at dawn?" Peter asked.

"I'd like you, Peter, to meet me first to check the boat. So, the plan is, I will come to your house and we go together. Once we make sure everything's okay with the boat, you can go to Arthur's house but I can't think of an idea for how you'd let Arthur know you're there without knocking on the door or the window," Billy's was thinking.

"I will keep my window open and I will look through it every now and then, until I see Peter," Arthur said.

"No, what if someone sees you?" Billy said.

"I've got an idea. When I arrive there, I can ring my bike's bell," Peter suggested.

"No, did you lose your mind? Everyone knows it's yours," Arthur said.

"What do you mean? I'm not the only one who has a bicycle," Peter said.

"Yes, but you're the only one who rings the bell of the bike without any reason," Billy said.

Billy and Arthur laughed at Peter.

"Guys, stop laughing at me… Hey, I got an idea," Peter said.

"What is it?" Arthur replied.

"I will make noises… Just don't worry. It's always meant to be quiet at the dawn… Once you hear those noises, you'd know it's me and you have to get out."

"What type of noises?" Arthur wondered.

"You can just count on me, okay?" Peter said.

Arthur shrugged his shoulders "Okay," he said.

"Arthur, I want to ask you one more time… Are you sure you won't tell your mother about the trip? Is this your last decision?" Billy asked.

"Yes. Yes, this is it. I will keep my promise, I won't tell her I'm only going to Shellia while I am actually going to Oernatus after it, I can't lie more." Arthur said.

"I understand."

"Shall we go? I'm hungry. We can talk about more details tomorrow. We still have a few days until Saturday arrives," Peter said,

"I agree," Arthur said.

"Yes, let's go," Billy said.

While Arthur was walking back home and said goodbye to Billy and Peter, his heart got pinched by the whole idea.

I have many reasons of not wanting to go and one of the main reasons is fear. I am scared and I have to admit it in my mind yet not to speak it out loud. I am afraid of traveling again, I am afraid of dying, I am afraid I would never come back home and my mother be by herself all alone. She only has me… Yes, she got her brother but he, his wife and child are not living with us. They have their own house and life. My mother only has me. And the thing that I am afraid the most of is that I would regret the whole thing if I'd go there and I found out my father wasn't there. At that point, I'd not believe in something called 'hope.'

Arthur knocked on the door and his mother opened the door for him quickly. Before she said a word, he could see her eyes speaking how worried she was about him for coming home late. He knew she'd ask him questions and she'd tell him how worried she was… She was his mother and she was everything to him. He didn't want to risk his life and neither wanted her to worry; *But it'd be amazing if I'd get to meet my father and bring him back home. I want to make my mother the happiest and I know she'd be like that only if my father was with us now. My heart tells me he's alive and he should be.*

I think I will risk my life one last time and my heart… you should be assured to be right this time, thought Arthur.

14- Party of Three

It should be the time… It was just right before dawn and Peter should show up in any minute now. Arthur still didn't know how he'd call him without being seen or caught. *He just didn't tell me and he told me 'Let it be a surprise.' What's wrong with this guy?* Arthur wondered.

Sometimes in serious situations, Peter would panic a lot and sometimes, he would take it easily and in a fun way. Arthur just hoped he'd not mess up the whole plan.

Arthur kept one window open and he waited while sitting on his bed. He prepared everything; his bag and the letter. He placed the letter on his pillow. He couldn't sleep for more than an hour. The idea of leaving without letting his mother know kept him sleepless most of the night. He wrote the letter at night with a dim light.

I hope she'd understand me and wouldn't get upset from what I am about to do, thought Arthur.

Without Arthur's awareness, he was tapping the floor with his foot the whole time while he was thinking. He stopped himself, he prayed that his mother didn't hear or feel it. Wooden floors surely would make noises. He just didn't understand how absent-minded he was sometimes, to the point he didn't even feel the taps that he made.

He finally heard a sound but this was strange and he was not quite sure if it was Peter for real. It was a sound of a cat meowing. *I don't think we had a cat around in the neighborhood, or could it be… Peter?* He got up and looked outside from his window but he didn't see any cat or anyone. Once Arthur looked away from the window and was about to sit down on the bed again, the meowing got louder and he returned to look from the window again. He finally saw Peter was hiding behind the garbage bin making this noise. Arthur covered his mouth before he would burst into laughter and looked away.

He slapped his cheeks and pulled them in order not to allow a laugh or a smile. That was very unexpected and funny for him. He managed to not laugh and it was time to leave. He picked up his bag and he slowly exited through the window. He couldn't believe he was doing this. He sighed and he walked stealthy toward Peter.

"Let's go," Peter said in the lowest tone he could speak with.

They kept walking carefully; now and then, Arthur looked back at his house, slowly fading as they got far away from it.

May God be with you, Mother, I will be back, Mother. I will come back, I promise.

They went to the east side of the port through the houses, where the area was mostly quiet and where the owned boats by families were kept. Normally, the owners wouldn't travel this early. The other side of the port was an active area where ships and fishermen boats were at. It could begin to be in action soon. So, Arthur and his friends must get moving quickly too. Billy was standing near the boat and he was looking around. If someone ever saw them, people would think they were up to something bad.

"Hey, put your bag in quickly," Billy said in a quiet voice.

Arthur put his bag on the boat. The boat looked not too big and not too small; it looked a little old but still in a good shape.

"Get on the boat, come on," Billy told Arthur quietly.

"Why are you guys whispering like this? Tell me the truth, guys, you didn't tell your family about this trip, did you? If you didn't, I am not going anywhere with you," Arthur replied.

"Shush now," Peter said.

"We did tell our families but you did not, Arthur. We have to be careful for you. That's all," Billy replied.

"Exactly like he said; my family knows I am going to Shellia today but not at this time though. Just get on the boat already," Peter said in a low tone.

"I see… Thank you, guys, for doing this for me," Arthur said quietly and he finally got on the boat.

Billy untied the rope; he and Peter pushed the boat and jumped in order to get on the boat. Billy started to sail the boat in the dark. The sun hadn't risen up yet but they could see an orange and red lines in the black sky, the sun was almost about to open its eye. Once they got a bit far from the port, they lighted up two lamps in order to see where they were heading to. He looked at the compass and looked around.

"I think this should be our way," Billy said.

"What do you mean you 'think'?" Peter was worried.

"I mean it is for sure the right direction," Billy tried to comfort Peter.

"Did you just change your words now? Guys, I don't want to be hunted down by a pirate," Peter said.

"Shh Peter, just trust me. I know where we are going and in case if we get lost… We surely would find another place to stay," Billy said.

"Right, we won't be forever in the seas wandering around the whole time," Arthur spoke.

"It is worse for me to sail in the dark…" Peter said and threw up in the sea.

Arthur forgot to bring ginger and honey for Peter. And Peter himself forgot to bring any. This voyage would be surely tough for him. *I hope he can pull himself together and stay still until we arrive to Shellia.*

Billy and Arthur suggested for Peter to lie down and sleep instead of sitting and looking around. He listened to what they reckoned and he lay down. It took him a long while to fall asleep but at least he was sleeping now. It was morning already; the sun had come up from under those curvy waves. It made Arthur wonder if his mother had found his letter and read it already… Thinking of how was she reacting to it, he prayed that she was alright.

Dear Mother,

I never thought I would write you a letter too soon in my life because I thought I wouldn't leave you ever. Don't worry, Mother, I am not leaving forever. Don't panic, my dear mother, I will just travel again but I didn't tell you because I promised you that I will never lie to you. I know leaving without letting you know is not any better than lying…

But you might wonder why am I being secretive about it? Well, I am going to a place that you would surely stop me from going. So, if I must go there, I should lie to you and I cannot do it, because I promised you. I feel if I lie one more time to you, a curse would fall upon me. I know no curse will fall but seeing you angry, it would make me imagine a thunder's hitting my heart and the trust between us would be splitting up in two halves like a tree after a thunder storm.

Mother, I do not want to worry you more but I am going to Oernatus; yes, Oernatus, and I am not going by myself, my friends Billy and Peter are with me. Mother, my heart is telling me my father is there. I will come back home with him. He might be a prisoner, or someone took him somewhere. I'd figure it out and we would come back. We will live happily like we used to. Mother, pray for me because your prayers strengthen me, protect me, and guide me.

I am sorry for not telling you this in person and writing you this letter instead. Forgive me, Mother, and I know when I come back, you would hold me in your protective arms.

Your only son,
Arthur

The sun was too yellow and a little pale orange. It looked like a yolk without its white. Arthur got hungry from seeing the sun this way. They had breakfast a while ago, and then they ate all the apples they had. It had been a long journey, Peter looked at his pocket watch and almost seven hours had passed already and they hadn't arrived yet. They didn't see Shellia from afar or any trace of it. They must have been still far or lost their way. Peter was panicking again, thinking they were lost. Arthur began to worry as well because it was only them, alone, with this old boat in the middle of the ocean, in the middle of nowhere. It was frightening.

The weather of the end of July was burning. They were sweating to the knees, it felt like the sun was grilling them up like fish. Their skins were too red like blood and they already were running out of water. They drank all of it. Peter took his shirt off a while ago and his back had some sunburn lines while Billy had unbuttoned all the buttons of his shirt. Arthur was the only one still wearing his shirt, thinking that his shirt would absorb his sweat but he felt itchy and soaked. Then he just took it off too.

"Why it is taking too long to arrive there? I am thirsty and starving. I feel sick," Peter was yelling.

"Calm down, this is an old boat. It is slower than other boats," Billy replied.

"Why didn't you tell us about this little information? I hate slow boats. I say it one more time, I HATE SLOW BOATS." Peter stood right before Billy and was not letting him look at the way.

"Your breath smells horrible, why don't you just sit down back there and let me concentrate on the way?" Billy was angry too.

"I won't and guess what, my breath is not the only thing that smells bad; you smell too fishy," Peter said.

Billy got up from his seat and one of his eyebrows rose, he glared at him as dangerous as a tiger.

"You are too loud. shut up and let me concentrate, you little spoiled kid," Billy said.

Peter stepped up closer to Billy. He stood on his toes, trying to be as almost height as Billy, his forehead was almost touched Billy's forehead.

"What did you just call me? Aren't you supposed to be the spoiled kid with a golden spoon in his mouth?" Peter said.

"Guys, stop. Don't fight," Arthur got up and he place his hand on Billy's shoulder. "It's hot, we're hungry and thirsty but fighting will only make everything worse."

"Don't be the good kid now, Arthur. Don't be nosy," Peter said.

"Peter, Billy, please don't fight in the middle of ocean... What if one of you fell off? I do not want to lose another friend. Please stop," Arthur said.

Peter and Billy became quiet for a few moments as they remembered Robert. Arthur looked behind Peter and he saw a land. It is far away but it was almost visible enough.

"Guys, look there." Arthur pointed toward it. "It must be Shellia."

Billy sat on his seat holding the wheel tight, Peter and Arthur stood behind him. They couldn't just sit anymore out of excitement. The more they got closer, the more they became impatient.

After almost an hour, they arrived there, Peter wore his shirt, Arthur did too, and Billy buttoned up his shirt. They took their bags and they walked through the port. Everyone there greeted them and welcomed them but Arthur and his friends' eyes captured a big tank of water and were only looking at it. Two sailor men were drinking from it but once they saw them, they pulled chairs for them to sit and offered wooden mugs to drink water.

"You must be exhausted; where did you come from?" one of the sailors asked.

Arthur and his friends were busying drinking water. They had never been this thirsty ever before.

"Another one, please," Peter said while he was handing his mug to a young man who was standing near the tank.

"Oh yes, sure," the young guy politely said. He wasn't even working there and he poured some water for him.

Peter was too dehydrated, he had vomited several times, his body was full of sun burns, and he was already out of breath. Thankfully, he made it in one piece.

"Sorry, sir. We came from Lillianta but sadly our boat was too slow," Billy took a deep breath after drinking lots of water.

"That's a shame. You should have come by a ship. It'd have been easier," the sailor replied.

"You're totally right. We only decided to sail by ourselves, but we never knew the hardship we'd face with an old boat," Billy said.

"It's okay, you gentlemen rest for a while here and drink enough water. Don't rush it. You look too tired to even walk, you must be dehydrated. Don't force yourself to walk right away," the sailor advised them.

"Well said. Thank you, sir," Billy said.

The two sailors left. Arthur and his friends stayed resting in the port and this young guy also excused himself shortly after and left. Peter finally began to breathe normally and calmed down. They sat for a while here under these shades of the great gate, while a little cool breeze blew.

Arthur sighed.

"Should we leave?" Billy asked them.

"Yes, I guess. Do you agree, Arthur?" Peter replied.

"Yes, let's go and find somewhere to eat and rest," Arthur said.

Billy nodded his head and they picked their bags and walked together. While they were walking, Peter out of blue said, "Sorry."

Billy looked at him. "Did you say something?"

"I said I am sorry," Peter looked at Billy.

"I am sorry as well," Billy apologized too.

Arthur smiled. He was glad that they were alright again. He had never seen them fighting like this before but he knew their hearts were filled with kindness and that they would apologize to each other soon.

They walked for a little more and suddenly they stopped and Arthur bumped into Billy.

"Guys, why did you stop?" Arthur asked.

Billy and Peter were looking at their left. Peter took off his hat. It was a place where it had tall walls with a sign written in big letters; in Kourtch language and a small translation in Lilliantian language; 'Graveyard'.

Arthur understood now what it was going through their minds. They were probably remembering Robert's funeral that was held in Shellia. They were probably remembering when they buried him. This… This touched Arthur deeply, he suddenly felt cold and he was shaking to the bones. He couldn't hold himself back.

Billy looked back at him and Arthur quickly looked down at his feet. Billy put his hand on Arthur's head and Arthur couldn't hold it back anymore; he was over, he was done, the tears were dropping off his face. Peter placed his hand on Arthur's shoulder. He was crying too.

"It is okay to cry," Peter said and sniffed.

"Do you want to visit him, pals?" Billy asked.

"It's okay for me but if Arthur doesn't feel ready, we can come here later," Peter wiped his tears with his arm.

"I am… I am okay." Arthur wiped off his tears. "I want to pray for him and maybe speak to him too."

"Okay, stand tall, guys. Let's go together," Billy said.

They entered the graveyard. The atmosphere felt dark, Arthur felt the day was turning into night, the weather from hot to chilly, when in fact, the sun was still up there, the weather was hot.

They reached Robert's grave but there was a young lady talking to his grave. "… I only loved you, Robert. My eyes were only looking at you, my love," she stopped once she felt their existence. She stood up and turned to look at them. Her eyebrows rose and her mouth was open, she was shocked to see them.

"You guys… The three of you now," Lousina spoke then she looked at Arthur and her sight narrowed just at him; her face expression was numb. From the way she looked at him, he understood she didn't want him to be around.

"Hello, Lousina," Peter broke the silence.

"Hi," Billy said.

"H-Hello," Arthur spoke at last.

Lousina nodded her head. "I should be going now. Come stop by to eat if you're hungry," she said.

"We'll see you around," Billy replied.

"See you," Arthur and Peter said.

She left and they prayed together for Robert. After a while, Arthur asked the guys to wait for him outside for little while, because he had some things to tell Robert.

He was standing all alone and his shadow was over Robert's grave. He got down and stayed low and he caressed his grave.

I can't believe he is under this mud. I can't believe he is gone this fast; it feels like yesterday, the last time that I saw him.

"Robert… I don't know but they said d-dead people c-can listen," he was choking with the words. "I miss you. I am not sad or angry at the fact that you stepped on my hand and let me fall off but I am upset and mad because you're gone. I sometimes think if I didn't survive, we would be together in this same graveyard. I wouldn't mind it, because we would keep accompany. But I am still alive and I am suffering from this heaviness in my heart whenever I wanted to talk with you or hang out with you I couldn't reach you… However, this heaviness has become less in my chest as I am talking with you now. I think I will come often to Shellia, to speak with you."

He wiped his tears and he sighed. He turned back, he saw that Peter and Billy were waiting for him, they looked exhausted. *I shouldn't keep them waiting longer than this.*

"Brother… I will go for now. Peter and Billy are waiting for me. Until next time, until next time… Bye for now, Robert."

After visiting Robert's grave, they went to the same restaurant where Lousina worked at. They ordered lots of food and they ate more than their need.

The time passed quicker than they expected it to. The time was just too slow when they were sailing toward here. It was already seven o clock but the sun didn't set yet. As usual, summer days lasted long. Arthur felt too exhausted. He had worked too much before in the tannery but he was never this exhausted ever before.

They paid for their meals and they stayed in the restaurant resting for a while. Lousina came to them holding a can in her hand.

"Guys, got a minute?" Lousina asked.

"Yes," Peter replied.

Lousina put the can on the table.

"Here, this is a paste for your sunburns. It is made out of honey and sesame oil and other natural ingredients."

"Thank you, it's kind of you," Billy said.

Arthur and Peter thanked her as well.

"It is nothing. You're staying until tomorrow, right?" Lousina asked.

"We're leaving early morning," Peter answered.

"You're going home too soon?" Lousina asked.

"No, we are going to…" Peter almost spilled the beans.

Arthur hit Peter with his elbow to stop him.

"I mean, we will probably go back home but we might stay another night because we're already tired and-and I think staying another day would be good to see around. Yeah." Peter said.

"I understand. By the way, do you have a place to stay for the night? If you don't, my uncle owns a small hotel and it has baths as well," Lousina said.

"Is it far from here?" Billy asked.

"No, not really. It is very near actually; if you're ready to go, I can guide you to it," Lousina said.

"We can go, yeah? I can't wait to bathe and sleep," Peter said.

"Alright, follow me," Lousina said.

Lousina walked ahead of them and it only took them a few minutes to arrive to the hotel. They booked a room for three; however, the room for three was not available. Instead, they arranged another room for them and brought an extra bed and they allowed them to access the baths until the room would be ready.

Arthur and his friends thanked Lousina again for her help, then they excused themselves to go to the baths. There were only two baths and Arthur had to wait. He went back to the lobby. Lousina hadn't left yet and she looked at Arthur. She came toward him.

"I have to go but it is a good chance to speak with you, Arthur," Lousina said.

Arthur avoided looking at her in the eyes. "What is it?" he asked.

"It is regarding Robert. I want to know…" she paused. "I want to know how your last conversation with Robert was like?" Lousina asked.

"Why?" Arthur asked and looked at her.

"Just tell me please," Lousina insisted.

He looked down again. "I remember I was going to bed but he stopped me and asked me if I didn't mind to talk with him for a short time. We stayed on the deck of the ship. I asked him if he was okay, he told me he was tired. He sighed and then finally told me about the fight he had with his brother because of drinking. And how he would reach out for alcohol when he'd not be feeling alright. I told him he could tell me what was wrong and maybe talking could help him to be better instead of drinking but he just got angrier and once I was about to leave, he asked me for forgiveness." As Arthur was telling her, he felt he was standing there with Robert on the deck and he went silent for a few seconds.

"He asked you for forgiveness? Then what?"

"I told him he didn't do anything wrong to me though but he insisted to hear the words 'I forgive you' from me and I did."

"That was it?"

"Yes, then I told him not to be late so he could find a good spot to sleep on. I left to sleep."

"Is it true he stepped on your hand or pushed you off?"

Arthur sighed. "Yes." He paused for a moment. "I was trying to climb up the ship after I tripped, and he stepped on my hand… I just fell down into the ocean."

"I am sorry…"

"It has nothing to do with you. Don't be sorry," Arthur replied.

"No, I want to confess about something," Lousina said.

"What… what is it?"

"It's my fault. I want you to forgive me too…"

"I don't understand… how is it your fault?"

"The last time I saw Robert, I was upset with him. He promised he'd visit me more often and I didn't see him for three weeks. He told me he would meet my family soon and propose but he didn't. I thought about the idea to make him jealous. And you were there… It was the first time I saw you and I thought… I would try to flirt with you or say anything to you that would make him jealous. Just so he'd take our relationship seriously. I was tired of waiting." She started to weep.

Arthur took a napkin out of his bag and handed it to her.

"Thanks... And he thought I liked you but I swear to God that I only had him in my heart. I told him before he'd leave that I was only trying to make him jealous. He forgave me and he became calm but he looked quite upset of what I had done and he decided to go back home with you guys. He said everything will be alright and I will come back soon. I didn't want him to leave while he was sad, it made my heart b-break... Then I received the news that he was dead, I felt I was dead too."

Arthur stood there silent and not knowing how to respond to her.

I kind of guessed that Robert liked Lousina from the moment he got angry when she said to me 'You're a shy guy.' I honestly didn't feel anything toward her and there is no way I'd get near my friend's girl.

"I am sorry, Arthur," Lousina said.

"I don't know what to say, Lousina. But I forgive you. I can see you're already being hard on yourself and blaming yourself. But, stop... I don't think Robert would like to see you in pain. You said he forgave you and he was willing to come to see you... Robert actually told me before that he was in love."

"He did?" Lousina broke down.

"Yes, he loved you. I am sure he doesn't want you to be still hurting."

"Thank you for telling me all this. Thank you... for your words. I think I should go now," Lousina was still crying.

"Take care."

"You too."

After a while, Peter and Billy were done bathing. Billy mentioned about going to buy some stuff for tomorrow. Arthur went to take a bath; it was too refreshing and resting. He didn't want to leave the bath too soon.

I could stay in here forever but of course, I can't, he thought. He was done bathing and he applied some of the paste that Lousina gave to them on his face and on his arms. He got dressed up and took his bag and went to the lobby but he didn't see his friends there. He asked the man who worked there and he told him their room was ready and they went there to rest.

Arthur went to the room and knocked on the door; Billy opened the door for him and Peter was already sleeping. Billy lay down on his bed and continued reading a book. Arthur sat on the empty bed. The room was quite small and there was a single window. He was glad his bed was near the window. Right way, he looked through the window behind the glass. He still admired Shellia even though it brought him a sort of sadness too. He looked around in the room and saw paper bags filled with fruit and food.

I guess Billy did a quick shopping for us because Peter seems like he had been sleeping for a while already. Billy was always thoughtful, good at planning and managing time.

Arthur finally lay down on his bed and he stared at the ceiling. His mind as usual was running into different thoughts, mainly he thought about the shell. He got up and he took it out of the bag. He listened to it and it still spoke the same thing.

"Hey, Arthur, throw it to me," Billy said.

Arthur threw it to him and he caught it. He put it against his ear and listened to it. Then he looked at it and said, "It has to be true. This must be real."

"Yes." Arthur replied.

"Tomorrow is going to be the day. We should sleep now in order to wake up early to go to Oernatus," Billy threw the shell back to Arthur and he caught it.

"By the way, do you know where it is? Did you find an old map?" Arthur asked.

"Not really, but I heard it would be not far from Shellia, in the north western," Billy said.

"That is what I heard too. But… but what if we don't find it?" Arthur said.

"We could sail for two or three hours. If we find nothing, we'd return to Shellia, stay for a night, then return back home," Billy said.

"Alright," Arthur replied.

"As far as I know, Oernatus should be near. We'll see though," Billy said.

"Yes," Arthur said.

Peter started to snore.

"This guy is surely in a deep sleep. Close your eyes and sleep too. I will blow off the lantern," Billy said.

"Okay, goodnight," Arthur said.

"Goodnight," Billy replied.

15- Delusion

Arthur got up to Billy's voice; he was calling Peter in order to wake him up but it was Arthur who woke up first. Poor Peter, he was still snoring. It was still dark outside, so was the room. The lantern only gave out a dim light, probably it was running out of oil. All of a sudden, Peter got up shaking, as if he had seen a nightmare.

"What? What…?" Peter gasped.

"Sorry, I didn't mean to scare you," Billy said.

"Are you okay?" Arthur asked.

Peter looked around and looked at them.

"Yes, I am okay. I just had a nightmare," Peter said and he rubbed his eyes.

"What time is it?" Peter asked.

"I didn't bring my watch. Where's your watch?" Billy asked.

"I don't know, maybe it is in my bag. I will check where it is," Peter said.

Peter got up and searched in his bag; he found his pocket watch.

"It is quarter past four. Are you leaving at this time?" Peter wondered.

"What do you think, Arthur?" Billy asked.

"I don't know, we can go if you're ready," Arthur replied.

"I honestly don't want to go at this time. I have to admit I have a bad feeling about going there; there is no shame in telling the truth and the truth is I am scared," Peter said.

"I am also afraid but I believe there would be an exciting adventure behind it," Billy said.

"What if we only find horror from such adventure?" Peter said.

Horror was the word; Arthur knew what it meant when he faced the ocean monster. He wasn't sure what he would see.

He thought, *Yes, I said I will do anything as I want to see everything to believe such tales are real… I just want to reach my father after all these years. There must be some reason why people keep avoiding going to Oernatus. Is it horror? Or is it just because of the history of wars that we had against them? Does this also mean if we arrive there, they'd kill us? There are so many questions in my mind but I have no answers. The answers can only be found when we go there.*

"Arthur, you didn't say anything," Billy asked.

"We came all this way for a reason or… reasons. We got tired, we sweated, we got sunburns, we got dehydrated… We risked our lives as we traveled by ourselves in an old boat. I know we shouldn't risk our lives further than this but we are just one step closer to finding out a new place, something new… They need our help too. I can't turn my back when someone asks me for help, that's how I was raised. This is my answer but I don't know if you are going to agree or not, though," Arthur said.

"You're right. What do you say, Peter?" Billy asked.

"I will go with you guys but let's wait for sunrise, at least; I don't want us to sail in this darkness. For our safety's sake," Peter said.

"Yes, I agree with Peter," Arthur said.

"Me too," Billy agreed.

Meanwhile, they decided just to eat. Billy had bought some food yesterday; they opened the paper bags and there was some bread, some cheese, and peaches. The bread was hard, but surely it was soft and warm when it came out of the oven. It was better than nothing really. They wouldn't find any market or restaurant open at such a time like this. They chattered about Peter's family business and the work they did during the week and how Arthur was lucky to work making bags and belts and how he was enjoying it better than working in the tannery. Billy was just listening to them and laughing about the fact how Peter still complained about the smell in the tannery. At least, the business had widened and things had got much better for them.

The time had come and Arthur could hear his heart beats racing. *It is now or never. Finally, I will get all the answers which were hidden in torn history books, the mysteries behind the shell... I cannot wait to see and find out even though there are many reasons and voices in my head that want to pull me back from taking this step but I won't let them control me. I must be brave, even for just this one time...*

They packed their stuff and left the hotel. It was very calm and the city was quiet. The streets seemed to be empty. They walked together; the company itself gave strength to each of them. Arthur knew the guys were worried; this was the first time they'd do something that their family didn't know about and were putting their lives in danger as well. They were not sure if Oernatus still existed and they had doubts where it was located; however, they were still going there. They reached the port and they only saw a few sailors there that they were still in their boat and ships. They assumed that they were probably just getting ready and waiting for people or their crew.

Arthur and his friends hurried up to avoid any conversations with the other sailors. They got on the boat and set sail right away. They first headed in a straight direction, so nobody would know where they were heading to, and then they turned west.

Billy was checking his compass. Peter lay down and covered his eyes with his arm, trying to avoid looking at the ocean waves in order not to get sick. They sailed for about two hours and they didn't see anything. Billy changed his direction to north west.

The weather was sunny and calm; however, the waves didn't seem to calm no matter what the weather was. After another hour, the weather started to chill and it was foggy. They sailed slowly, lighted up a lamp, and Arthur and his friend stood alert, looking around. It got really frightening. Arthur felt he was living the dream he saw a few days ago. His heart sank and he couldn't say a word.

Slowly, the boat stopped.

"What happened?" Peter panicked.

"I don't know… the boat is not working. Don't worry, I will try to fix it," Billy said.

"Do you know how to fix it? Hey, what are you going to do if it does not work again?" Peter asked.

"Calm down, let me focus here," Billy said while checking the boat.

"It feels chilly, or is it only me?" Arthur said while rubbing his shoulders.

"It is little bit cold," Peter said.

A strong wind blew and they knelt down... the boat started to sail backward because of the wind. They got up and tried to remove the sail cloth. As they were busy folding it, the wind calmed and once they looked around, all they saw was ice. The waves were frozen, the water was frozen, the ocean itself was frozen. As if the time stopped, as if they entered a different world. There was frozen dew over their bodies. Their faces didn't have an expression; just too pale and too shocked to even say a word.

"Do you... Do you see what I see?" Peter asked and sat down on his knees.

Arthur failed to speak up.

"Do you see what I see? CAN YOU HEAR ME?" Peter shouted and his voice echoed.

"Yes... Everything is frozen, how this is even possible?" Billy asked and looked at Arthur, thinking that he'd have an answer.

Peter got up and shook Arthur.

"Arthur, say something," Peter said.

Arthur grabbed Peter's hands, pushed them off, and made him stop.

"I just... I am too shocked. We are stuck in the middle. The boat is not working and I am afraid to die, freezing here; that's the last thing I expected," Arthur said.

"Shush, Arthur... Don't say such a thing," Billy said and returned to repairing the boat. "We will get there; nothing will stop us."

"No, when the boat works, let us go home. I don't want to continue," Peter said.

"Arthur, say something... Don't just agree with him, we came all the way for this. We shouldn't stop now," Billy spoke.

I don't know who I should agree with. My mind has blown away with the wind, with everything I see now. All I feel is fear. I don't know if I have the strength to continue. Peter is shivering from the chilly weather; his lips are trembling and I can't feel my hands.

"Arthur!" Billy called Arthur.

"Yes... yes... I don't know. Don't talk with me right now, please, I can't think of anything. Let's just hope the boat works again," Arthur said.

The boat made a huge noise, it started to crack. It was slowly breaking; the boat couldn't handle the ice.

Suddenly, they heard a man shouting. He called them with their names. They looked behind them and saw a big boat and a group of men. Arthur tried to look carefully and saw one of them was Kevin.

"Guys, it is Kevin," Arthur said.

"Indeed, it is Kevin. Hey! Hey, come over here. Help us!" Peter shouted and his shout echoed.

"Hang on," Kevin said in loud voice and his voice echoed.

The boat got closer and stopped near their boat and they threw a wooden ladder for them to climb up.

"Thank God, you came to help us. The boat is cracking up because of the ice," Peter said while he climbed up.

"What ice?" Kevin asked.

Arthur gestured for Billy to go before him and he climbed the ladder.

"What do you mean? Don't joke with us. The ocean is frozen," Billy said and got on the boat.

"I seriously don't see any ice. What are you talking about?" Kevin was surprised and he looked at the other men who were with him.

They mumbled, "What ice? What are they talking about?"

Arthur looked around him and he saw the water was frozen. *Why Kevin can't see the ice? Is this a delusion? This can't be.* He touched the water and it was literally ice.

"You are surely joking, Kevin?" Arthur said.

"I am not, you think I have time to joke... Come on, Arthur, get up. You guys are already in a danger zone, we must leave," Kevin said.

Arthur began to think, *This is it... This could be the mystery behind Oernatus. This is why people wouldn't go to it. It must be strange but I think if I walk over the ice, I will surely reach Oernatus. It is like a puzzle about to be solved. If I walk over it, I will reach the shore. All I need is courage and I should gain it now.*

"Guys, the shell is real and the ice is real too... I am no way backing off from this. I will give it a try. A final try. Don't worry about me. I will make it," Arthur said.

"Arthur! Stop! Arthur!" Billy shouted, his voice echoed!

He put his foot on the ice; he could feel it to be too strong and hard. *Yes, I can walk on it.* He added more pressure on the ice, so he'd finally stand with both of his feet but before he could even stand, his feet sank and he fell into the ocean.

I don't get what is going on, I am drowning again.

He looked up to the surface and he saw clear water... no ice.

What is going on? How the ice is gone? Why I am not swimming or moving? I should do something; I should swim and save myself.

His will to live was strong but his body seemed to forget to move. Bubbles were coming out of his mouth and he slowly closed his eyes.

Arthur thought his life, his story had come to an end; little did he know, it had just begun. Perhaps, he passed the test because there was something that was pushing him up to the surface. He woke up again but he kept fainting. The water was splashing on his face. Yet, he was unconscious. That mysterious creature had carried Arthur all the way to the shore.

The shores of Oernatus.

¬To be continued¬